Summer Rush

A Katana Bay Series

Katie Winters

ALL RIGHTS RESERVED. No part of this publication may be reproduced, distributed, or transmitted in any form or by any means, including photocopying, recording, or other electronic or mechanical methods, without the prior written permission of the publisher.

Copyright © 2023 by Katie Winters

This is a work of fiction. Any resemblance of characters to actual persons, living or dead is purely coincidental. Katie Winters holds exclusive rights to this work. Unauthorized duplication is prohibited.

Chapter One

This far from shore, it was easy for Janine to forget everything about her life— what had come before and what awaited her after. Weightless, the ocean breeze shimmying through her white dress and her long, gray-streaked hair, she flowed languidly across the sailboat, adjusting sails and ropes, following Henry's lead. For more than two years now, Henry had been her rock, her guide, and her love— an essential and powerful force after everything that had happened in the spring of 2021. And now, as his sailboat rocketed across the blue of the Nantucket Sound, he turned to her, took her hands in his, and said, "Baby, are we ever going to get married?"

The question brought Janine back down to planet earth. Laughing, she tossed her head and cuddled against him, overwhelmed with the promise of the approaching few months. When Henry had asked her to marry him, she'd agreed whole-heartedly. But that had been before both Maggie and Alyssa had gotten pregnant within months of one another, before Maggie and her husband had decided to divorce, and before another onslaught of chaos had come up to greet her, reminding her that, eternally, life was to be lived— and there was no rest for the weary.

"I love you, Henry," Janine breathed into his white shirt.

Henry kissed her on the cheek. "I love you, too." He paused. "Why do I get the hint there's a 'but' coming?"

"It's not a 'but,' exactly. It's just that, well. You know. The girls."

"The girls!" Henry laughed and sat down along the railing of the sailboat so that Janine could curl up beside him, then dropped anchor so that he could pour them two glasses of champagne. It was hard to believe it was August, the tail-end of yet another gorgeous summer on Martha's Vineyard. Winter seemed like an impossibility, something Janine understood in another life. But always, it approached, just like your next breath, and it was only a few months away now. And blissful summer days like this would feel just as impossible.

Janine accepted her glass of champagne and sipped, studying Henry's face for signs of anger and sorrow. But nothing like that was reflected back.

"I worry about them so much," Janine offered. "Especially now that Hunter is coming to get Lucy. They've taken such good care of that girl for the past year and a half, almost. Maggie especially has turned her life upside down for her."

"You don't have to explain it," Henry assured her, his tone slightly dark but his eyes soft, filled with assurance. "I know how much you love Lucy, too. She's been your stand-in granddaughter."

Janine blinked back tears. It was true what Henry said. In the spring of 2022, Alyssa's high school boyfriend, Hunter, had gone to rehab and left his beautiful toddler, Lucy, with Alyssa and Maggie. After he'd gotten out of rehab, they'd assured him they could care for Lucy until he was stable, with a steady income and a good place to live. For a little while, Janine, Maggie, and Alyssa had settled into the idea that Lucy was a part of their family now— not his. Until two weeks ago, when Hunter had made the call to say he was ready, healthy, and it was time for him to take Lucy back, to be the father she deserved. They'd wept for hours.

"I know it's a good thing," Janine said to Henry now. "I've known Hunter since he was a little kid, and I want the best for him. I certainly don't want him to miss out on his daughter's life."

"It will be difficult to say goodbye," Henry said gently. "But the three of you have done exactly what you set out to do. You've protected and loved that little girl. And Hunter will always be grateful."

Despite their distance from shore, Janine was surprised to feel her phone vibrating in her pocket. A glance at the screen told her it was her lawyer calling. This was a rare thing indeed, especially after her ex-husband, Jack's death of a heart attack back in November of 2021. After his affair with her best friend, an official divorce had never been necessary, although sometimes, Janine wished she'd legally distanced herself from him. What a messy time that had been.

"Go ahead and get that," Henry said breezily. "We have all day out here."

"It's probably just something insignificant, another tether to my old life. Maybe we finally sold that vacation house in Singapore. I don't know why Jack ever wanted to buy that in the first place," Janine offered.

But already, Henry reached for his paperback, a Jack London novel, and nodded at her phone. "Just answer it. Don't worry about me."

Janine sighed and forced herself from this world and into her lawyer's. "Hello? This is Janine speaking."

"Hello, Janine!" Janine's lawyer was named Mike Gladstone, and he was fast-talking and incredibly Manhattan, the type of man who would do anything for a buck and knew his way around the loopholes of the legal system with expert agility. This was why Jack had liked him so much, Janine knew. For her part, she'd never demanded he look for any loophole.

"I've just received some news," Mike went on. "Regarding your mother-in-law."

Janine arched her eyebrow. Jack's parents had never been particularly fond of her. In their eyes and the eyes of the rest of the world, she'd been a two-bit Brooklyn waitress Jack had picked up and impregnated. They'd always seen her as the floozy who'd ruined Jack's life.

"And by that, I mean Jack's biological mother," Mike went on excitedly.

"Teresa?" Janine's voice was higher than she'd planned for, but that was due to shock. In all her years of marriage to Jack, she'd never once met Teresa, his father's first wife, who'd been raised in Italy and then returned there after Jack's father's affair all those years ago. (Like father, like son.) Despite the circumstances, because Teresa had ultimately abandoned her son, Jack had never liked talking about her— and Janine hardly knew anything about her at all.

"Teresa Cacciapaglia," Mike affirmed. "She recently

passed away in her home in Venice, Italy. I'm sorry for your loss."

Janine struggled to comprehend why Mike would say he was sorry for her loss. Teresa was a stranger.

"She was really sick the past few years," Mike went on. "I don't think she was fully coherent when Jack died. She never updated her will to reflect his death, anyway. But, due to the legal wording in said will, it seems that everything that was supposed to go to Jack now goes to Maggie and Alyssa, Jack's only heirs."

Janine's jaw dropped. Henry closed his paperback and gave her a strange look.

"Um. What do you suggest we do?" Janine stuttered.

Mike laughed openly. "Well, let's see. I suppose, if I were you, I would head over to Venice to see the will and villa for yourself. Make a vacation of it. Heck, why not? Venice is probably the most romantic place in the world."

Janine's mind swirled with questions. On the one hand, both of her daughters were pregnant— Alyssa, nearly six months and Maggie, nearly four. But as long as the doctor cleared them for travel, it wasn't too late to fly over to Italy, was it? Plus, this would be their final vacation without babies, which was probably essential bonding time.

On top of that, going away would distract the three of them from Lucy's departure.

"I have to talk this over with my daughters," Janine said. "I'll call you later, okay?"

"Great," Mike answered. "And congratulations. Venice!"

As Janine hung up the phone, she rolled her eyes into the back of her head. She couldn't believe the lack of tact of her lawyer— congratulating her over the death of someone she hadn't ever known.

"What's up?" Henry demanded. "That conversation sounded serious."

Janine explained what she knew: that Teresa had passed away after a long illness and left her villa and estate to Alyssa and Maggie. That there were things to organize abroad, and it was essential that the three of them go and work it all out. As she spoke, Henry's eyes flickered from turquoise to green from the light of the ocean.

"Venice is incredible," he breathed. "And those old Italian homes are remarkable! Do you know how old it is?"

"Jack hardly ever talked about her," Janine reported, "but I always got the sense that Teresa came from a great deal of money— just like everyone in Jack's world— and that her family was very, very old."

"Hundreds and hundreds of years," Henry repeated.

"Uh oh," Janine said with a laugh. "I see the documentarian coming out in you. You're always looking for the next story."

"I know. I know. But the history of Italy is fascinating stuff, and you have a direct link to it. I wish I could sink my teeth into all you're about to learn."

"You're welcome to it," Janine offered. "If you want to make a documentary about my ex-husband's late biological mother, go for it."

Henry winced for a moment before he smoothed out his features, closed his book, and kissed her again. "I have some editing to do on the last shoot. It'll keep me busy as you gallivant through Venice with your daughters."

Janine's heart swelled. By contrast to her late

husband, Henry always seemed to understand exactly what she needed when she needed it, regardless of what he wanted.

"Why are you so good to me?" Janine breathed as she wrapped her arms around his waist.

"I should ask you the same thing," Henry said.

Janine pressed her nose into his chest. "I really will marry you, Henry," she said softly.

Her heart thudded at how serious she felt about this. When she'd learned of Maxine and Jack's affair, she'd sworn off love and marriage, assuming herself to be easily manipulated and even stupid for allowing herself to fall for someone like him. But now, just two years older and worlds wiser, she felt more in-tune with her soul and far more willing to forgive herself. It was funny what true love did to you. It gave you space to breathe.

Chapter Two

The six a.m. yoga session was quieter than usual. Several women at the Katama Lodge and Wellness Spa had checked out yesterday afternoon, headed back to their families, their work responsibilities, and, generally, the stressors that had sent them to the spa in the first place, leaving the Lodge drafty, battening down its hatches for the approaching hurricane season. Nancy Remington, the head yoga instructor and the mother of Janine, the Katama Lodge's head naturopathic doctor, stretched into a Downward Dog pose, her eyes half-open to watch the eight sleepy women follow her lead. "That's right," Nancy said gently. "Really focus on your breathing, here. Give yourself grace."

The yoga class ended at six-forty-five. Nancy stood at the exit, nodding to the women as they passed, smiling, and wishing them good luck for the rest of their stay. Normally after a session like this, Nancy went to her office, had a cup of coffee, caught up on emails, and prepared for the next yoga session at eight-thirty. But this morning, Nancy was needed back at home.

As Nancy sped through the office, still in her yoga pants, her hair streaming out behind her, her stepdaughter, Elsa, stepped out of her office looking similarly harried. She flashed a smile at Nancy and locked her office door.

"I can't believe today's the day," she said.

Nancy pressed her hand over her heart. "It's hard to believe."

"Our girl!" Elsa stepped in line with Nancy, hurrying toward the parking lot. "I take it Maggie isn't handling it well?"

"Neither of them are," Nancy said, speaking of her granddaughters, Alyssa and Maggie, who had to say goodbye to Lucy today.

"I'm picking up fresh orange juice on the way," Elsa said as she opened the door for Nancy. "Need anything else from the store?"

"We should be good," Nancy said. "See you at home."

In the front seat of her car, Nancy watched Elsa through the rear-view as she backed through the parking lot and sped out of sight. That summer, Elsa had moved in with her fiancé, Bruce Holland, which had created a distance between Elsa and the rest of the Remington women— probably one that was necessary in many ways. After Elsa's father, Nancy's husband, had died, Elsa had been reeling, nursing her wounds in the enormous home in which Neal had raised her and her sister, Carmella. It was invigorating for Nancy to watch Elsa rebuild her life and her heart. But it also made her sad not to have her close. It served as a reminder that Neal was gone, fully gone, and that life had to go on, one way or another, regardless of how Nancy felt about it.

In truth, she was beginning to feel like a little old lady whose story was coming to an end.

Nancy parked the car in the driveway of the Remington House and hustled inside, where she found Janine at the kitchen counter, Maggie in a kitchen chair with Lucy on her lap, and Alyssa leaning against the wall with a mug of tea.

"Grandma! Hi!" Maggie smiled, her eyes sparkling with tears.

"Grammy!" Lucy waved both of her hands and giggled. It was clear that she couldn't fully comprehend what was about to happen, that her father was on his way to the island to pick her up, and that this was her goodbye brunch.

"Oh, sweetie, good morning." Nancy kissed Lucy on the forehead and blinked back tears of her own. "It smells great, Janine."

"Eggs, bacon, blueberry pancakes, and yogurt with homemade granola," Janine said, speaking a little quicker than normal.

"I hope you're hungry," Alyssa said. "Mom made enough to feed a team of football players."

Janine blushed as Nancy hurried to say, "I can understand that. Sometimes, we need to put our nervous energy somewhere. Might as well put it in some pancakes."

"Apparently, there's even more to be nervous about," Alyssa went on. "Have you told Grandma, Mom?"

"Told me what?" Nancy asked, suddenly terrified: was Janine going to move out of the house? Were Alyssa and Maggie going to go back to the city? What would she do in this big place, all alone?

"I got a call from Jack's lawyer yesterday," Janine said. "Apparently, his biological mother died."

Nancy wrinkled her nose, never keen to hear anything about that scoundrel who'd cheated on her daughter. "And?" She felt impatient.

"He never really knew her," Janine explained. "After his father cheated on her, she left Jack behind and returned to Venice, where she lived mostly by herself until her recent death. Apparently, Alyssa and Maggie are her only next of kin."

Nancy's jaw dropped. This was a storyline she hadn't anticipated, not in her wildest dreams.

"There's a will," Maggie explained. "And Mom thinks we should head out there and check it out."

Lucy babbled to herself, then took a doll from the tabletop and swept her fingers through her blonde curls.

"It'll be a good distraction," Janine offered, raising her mug of coffee toward Lucy.

"I see," Nancy said. "When are you off?"

As Janine explained that Alyssa and Maggie had doctors' appointments before they left, just to clear them for travel, there was the sound of the front door opening, followed by Carmella's bright voice. "Good morning!" Afterward came her daughter, Georgia's coo of happiness.

"Morning!" Alyssa, Nancy, Janine, and Maggie answered in unison as Janine hurried to pour Carmella a mug of tea.

Carmella set Georgia up in her carrier in the next room, where she remained fast asleep, then sat across from Maggie, both hands on her stomach. Recently, she'd divulged the fact of her second pregnancy, which thrilled Maggie and Alyssa, as it meant Carmella's children would be approximately the same age as theirs. It boggled Nancy's mind sometimes to consider that Carmella had gotten pregnant with both of her children in her forties while Nancy had had her only daughter at the age of sixteen.

Not long afterward, Elsa came with the fresh orange juice, followed by Mallory, Elsa's daughter, and Aria, Cole's new girlfriend. Nancy swallowed all three of them with hugs and ordered everyone to sit at the outdoor table, with its glittering view of the ocean— a sight to see this early in the morning, before sunlight burned the sands and sent them indoors until evening.

Plates filled, the Remington women tucked in, breaking egg yolks, sliding toast through the orange, and drizzling syrup over pancakes. In a final moment of motherly love, Maggie sliced Lucy's pancakes and helped position the tiny plastic fork in Lucy's hand so that she could serve herself. It broke Nancy's heart to see it, an act Maggie had done hundreds of times at this point.

"It's hard to believe we won't see her every day," Maggie said, her voice very small as she watched Lucy dig into the pancakes.

Alyssa swept her napkin beneath her eye to catch a tear. "You should see the list Maggie made Hunter."

"What? He needs to know about his daughter! About how she likes her bedtime stories and how she eats her pears and..." Maggie trailed off and smiled to herself. "I realize I'm making it sound difficult. But in retrospect, taking care of Lucy was maybe the easiest thing in the world. She was always, always so good to us."

"And you were good to her," Janine said.

"I think we should go around the table and say a memory we have of Lucy," Elsa suggested.

Maggie's face crumpled. "I don't know if I'll be able to choose just one!"

"I can start," Nancy said, sensing Maggie was on the brink of breaking down. "It was last autumn when we took Lucy to the apple orchard for fresh donuts and cider."

"Oh!" Maggie crossed her arms tightly over her chest. "Her face was covered in cinnamon all day long! I couldn't get all of it off."

"I don't think Lucy wanted you to clean her up," Nancy said with a laugh. "She managed to get her hand on a cinnamon donut hole every few minutes, even sweet-talking the owner to get freebies."

"She learned how to manipulate. I think she got that from me." Alyssa eyed Lucy lovingly.

"I remember when you first brought her here," Janine said, "and you didn't know her name."

"We called her Cici," Maggie said, her voice breaking. "I couldn't believe how close her real name was!"

"It was like we could sense it," Alyssa offered, locking eyes with her sister.

Nancy's heart flipped over. Although she was close with her stepdaughters and closer than ever with Janine, she could never comprehend the love Alyssa and Maggie had for one another. They couldn't have been more different: Maggie with her urgent responsibilities and Alyssa with her fly-by-the-seat-of-her-pants mentality. Yet they loved one another endlessly, open-heartedly, with unlimited forgiveness and compassion.

Just after the Remington women finished swapping stories of Lucy's time with them, the front doorbell rang. All the color drained from Maggie's face as Alyssa snapped up, her hand over her pregnant belly.

"I guess that's him."

Alyssa disappeared into the house to fetch her high

school boyfriend, the only man in the world she'd ever loved, as far as Nancy knew. According to Janine, Hunter had been a wonderful part of Alyssa's life back in high school, and Janine had been sad when the two of them had broken up. A few months ago, Nancy had asked Janine if she thought Hunter and Alyssa would ever get back together, especially now that Alyssa had helped raise Lucy. Janine had said she wasn't sure. "I think the romance part of their story is finished, and maybe that's okay."

As the handsome and six-foot-tall Hunter stepped onto the back porch, his smile broke open at the sight of little Lucy.

"Daddy!" Lucy jumped from Maggie's lap and hurried to her father, whom she probably recognized more from video chats than from her own memories.

"Lucy!" Hunter lifted Lucy so that she could wrap her arms around his neck, then kissed her cheek, her forehead, his eyes sparkling. The reunion was so powerful that, eventually, Nancy had to look away. This man loved Lucy with everything. That was clear. But it didn't make saying goodbye to Lucy any easier.

For a little while, Hunter sat with them at the breakfast table with Lucy on his lap. Maggie continued to scrunch the fabric on her thighs as though she was nervous now that Lucy was held by someone else. Alyssa smiled at him with a mix of confusion and joy, probably remembering him as the first boy she'd ever loved, sensing that he'd come through time to disrupt her life.

Hunter said and did all the right things at breakfast that morning. He doted on Lucy, talked about his new job and girlfriend out in Seattle, and showed photographs of the new apartment he'd rented, complete with a decorated bedroom for Lucy.

"What does your girlfriend do, Hunter?" Carmella asked.

"She's in med school," Hunter answered proudly. "I've never seen anyone work harder in my entire life. That said, she took plenty of time off from studying just to help me prepare for Lucy. That paint color in Lucy's bedroom is obviously all her. I never would have gone for lilac." He laughed gently as Alyssa's cheeks turned a brighter shade of crimson.

Not long afterward, Hunter announced it was time for him and Lucy to go. Maggie stood, her face crumpling, then turned to the side so that Hunter and Lucy couldn't see her. Alyssa jumped forward to hug Hunter first, saying quietly, "Having Lucy was one of the greatest gifts of our lives. But she's missed her daddy. She needs you. I'm so glad you're ready for this, Hunter."

"I can't thank you all enough," Hunter said, his voice breaking. "I was in a dark place. A horrible place. I wasn't sure where to turn. And it's the biggest surprise of my life, maybe, that my high school girlfriend was the one who came through for me."

Blinking back tears, Alyssa swatted him on the upper arm as Maggie composed herself enough to approach and hug Hunter and then crouch down to shower Lucy with kisses.

"You be a good girl, Lucy. Okay? And we'll come out to see your new home soon. Okay?"

Lucy still seemed not to understand. Playfully, she grabbed Maggie's hand and led her to the living room, where Maggie and Alyssa had arranged two suitcases and a backpack mostly filled with diapers and stuffed animals.

The Remington women followed Alyssa, Maggie, Lucy, and Hunter into the living room, where, one after another, they hugged Lucy close and wished her well. It was not clear how much of this time Lucy would remember. Probably, all of it would be lost. Nancy wasn't sure how to deal with the devastation she was feeling, so she shoved it deep and smiled at Alyssa and Maggie lovingly. "You're stronger than you know," she whispered to Maggie, whose chin quivered.

But just after Alyssa and Maggie piled the suitcases into the back of Hunter's rental, and just after they kissed Lucy a final time and buckled her into her car seat, Lucy squealed with confusion. Her cheeks were blotchy, and her eyes were lined with red.

"Why aren't you coming?" Lucy demanded of Alyssa and Maggie with more authority than most three-year-olds should have been allowed.

Alyssa and Maggie held hands and spoked to Lucy quietly, again telling her what they'd told her perhaps ten times: that she was moving in with her father, that they would see her soon. But Lucy was inconsolable. Maggie squeezed her little hand, her shoulders shaking, as Alyssa kissed her cheeks and then locked eyes with Hunter.

"You should go," she said. "She'll be okay. We all will be."

Hunter was white as a sheet. He shut the door of the rental, which echoed with Lucy's wails, then got in the driver's seat and eased down the driveway. Even when he turned the corner down the block, Nancy could still make out the sounds of that little girl weeping.

After the car was out of sight, Maggie and Alyssa

turned and hugged one another, their eyes closed against the immensity of the moment. One after another, Janine, Elsa, Carmella, Mallory, and Nancy retreated into the house, sensing the girls needed space alone. In the kitchen, as Janine stacked the dishes in the dishwasher with shaking hands, Nancy cupped her elbow and whispered, "Take the girls to Italy."

Janine nodded. "It's the only way."

Chapter Three

A week later, Nancy found herself in the same position: saying goodbye to people she loved in the immense shade of the Remington House. A ravenous August sun shimmered overhead, and her body was slick with sweat from only a few minutes of packing up Janine's car.

"You three take care of yourself," Nancy ordered as she hugged each of them. "Eat plenty of pasta for me."

"Don't worry about that," Alyssa said. "I will not neglect the carbs in Italy."

Maggie rolled her eyes and slid into the passenger seat of Janine's car. "I pre-mixed everything I could for the bakery, but if you could…"

"Stop by and make sure everything's running smoothly?" Nancy smiled.

"I know. I know. I'm annoying myself with how many times I've asked you," Maggie said with a sigh.

"Everything is handled, Maggie," Nancy told her. "David and Heidi have the place running like a tight ship. But I'll make sure to go over there and check on them, if only to get a free chocolate chip cookie out of it."

"I appreciate that, Grandma," Maggie said with a laugh.

Last spring, Maggie had begun baking for The Dog-Eared Corner, a bookstore and coffee shop in Martha's Vineyard owned by an older woman named Heidi. When Maggie had found out about Heidi's estranged son, David, she'd dragged Alyssa to Manhattan to track him down at a bookstore, where he was signing copies of his novels. Eventually, she'd found a way to bring mother and son together again— and had even fallen in love with David herself. Their surprise pregnancy had come not long after they'd met.

"We'll be home soon," Janine said, hugging her mother a final time before jumping in the driver's seat.

Feeling foolish and very alone, Nancy remained standing in the driveway and waved to her granddaughters and daughter until they disappeared around the corner. For a moment, Nancy remained there, sweating in the August heat, until she turned to face the enormous house. Many decades ago, Neal had purchased it with his first wife, with the plan to raise their children in it. The house had been through countless periods of devastation since then. It had seen so much death, but it had persevered through so much goodness and beauty, as well. Since Janine's move from New York City, it had been the home to many, many members of the family— all of whom had come together for nightly dinners to gossip, laugh, and fuel themselves, despite their heartbreaks or the chaos of the rest of the world.

But now, despite all that had come before, Nancy found herself all alone in that house.

It felt wrong.

For a little while that morning, Nancy was able to distract herself. She paid bills, wrote in her journal, and watered her plants. But by noon, she was on the local humane society website, asking herself if she should go and get a cat or a dog. Never in her life had she had a pet. Maybe this was the right time?

Around three, Elsa called to ask if Nancy could teach a yoga lesson that evening. "Brenda is sick," Elsa explained, speaking of another yoga teacher, a recent hire.

"I'd love to!" Nancy leaped at it, embarrassing herself with how quickly she answered.

Nancy showered, changed into her yoga outfit, and sped off to the Katama Lodge, where she walked so quickly through the hallways that she nearly bumped directly into Carmella.

"Hi, Nancy!" Carmella smiled. "Did you send our girls off to Italy?"

"I did. I think I'll feel antsy until I hear they've landed," Nancy said. "I hate it when I can't reach them."

"Why don't we go out tonight?" Carmella suggested. "Maybe Elsa and I can keep your mind off of that."

Nancy felt nervous that Carmella and Elsa were going out of their way for her because they felt bad for her. Then again, this was Nancy's very first day alone in that big house— and she didn't want to be stuck there all night, wandering the hallways, checking her phone for messages from Janine.

"I'm sure you're tired," Nancy said, "with Georgia and the pregnancy and all."

"Come on," Carmella pushed it. "When was the last

time it was just you, Elsa, and I? You'd be doing me a favor. I'd love to catch up."

After yoga, Nancy changed into a black summer dress she kept at the Lodge, then met Carmella and Elsa in the lobby. Elsa's smile was exuberant, and she wrapped her arm around Nancy's shoulders and led her to the parking lot, suggesting wine bars and restaurants with gorgeous verandas, anything to fit the beauty of the night.

"Why don't we go to the Aquinnah Cliffside Overlook?" Carmella suggested. "I still haven't been there since they opened."

"Brilliant," Elsa said. "I'll drive."

The Aquinnah Cliffside Overlook Hotel had reopened that summer, eighty years after a hurricane had torn it apart. It suited a luxurious crowd, bringing in high rollers from the eastern seaboard for Michelin-star food, croquet, horseback riding, sailing, and cocktail parties that rivaled the best in the world (or so Nancy had read). As they entered the grand dining hall, they spotted the hotel owners, Xander Van Tress and Kelli Montgomery, at the head table, dining with Kelli's cousin, Susan Sheridan, and her husband, Scott. As they passed, Elsa, Carmella, and Nancy waved, with Elsa pausing for a moment to chat. Susan was Bruce's business partner at the law firm, a necessary part of Elsa's new life with her new love. As Nancy and Carmella were seated at a table in a sunbeam to study the menus, Elsa and Susan's laughter echoed through the enormous hall.

Nancy and Elsa both ordered glasses of rosé, while Carmella opted for a mocktail meant to taste like an Aperol Spritz.

"I'm so glad we could do this," Elsa said, her glass

raised. "Nancy, I have to admit, I've thought about you in that big house by yourself during the girls' trip."

"I've hardly ever been there alone," Carmella said, wrinkling her nose. "When I was younger, I was convinced it was haunted."

Nancy laughed and waved her hand. "It's bizarre to be there by myself. Stranger, too, when I think about when I first was dating your father. He brought me there, and I just couldn't fathom how enormous it was. Now, all those rooms are mine?" She shook her head. "It doesn't feel quite right. In fact, if it weren't for Alyssa and Maggie and the approaching babies, I'd consider downsizing."

"You're going to need plenty of space," Carmella affirmed.

"That house is ready for another generation," Elsa said. "It's what Dad would have wanted."

Nancy sipped her rosé, stirring with a mix of sorrow and longing. Throughout her marriage to Neal, he'd never once met Janine or her grandchildren. She felt as though she'd lived many lives, none of which connected.

"You'll never guess what happened today," Carmella began, her eyes dancing. "Another near-acupuncture disaster!"

"Oh no!" Elsa cried.

As Carmella explained what had happened during a session with a particularly impatient woman, Nancy's eyes roamed from the table toward a man a few seats away. He was maybe a few years older than she was, with olive-tone skin and dark green eyes, and he was staring at her in a way that made her stomach twist into knots. Nancy forced herself to blink away, to focus again on what Carmella said. But when she checked on him again, she found that his staring had grown even more intense.

There could be no mistaking it. She was all he could look at right now.

Nancy cupped her hand over her mouth and spoke very quietly. "Carmella? I'm sorry to interrupt."

"What's wrong?" Carmella frowned.

"That man over there is staring at me?" Nancy breathed.

Before she could stop them, both Elsa and Carmella twisted around to gaze at the man a few tables away. Caught red-handed, the man smiled at them, showing too many very white teeth. He then raised his glass of red wine toward them and said, "Good evening."

"Evening!" Elsa raised her glass in return while Nancy kept hers on the table.

"This is a fabulous hotel," the man said, his accent lilting. It was clear he wasn't a native English speaker, although Nancy couldn't have said where he was from. Maybe somewhere in Europe? Italy?

"Are you staying here?" Carmella asked.

"I'm not," the man said. "I rented an entire house on the coast a little ways from here. Although I must say, it's a bit lonely, being in that house all by myself. Maybe I should have rented a hotel room instead."

Carmella flicked her gaze back toward Nancy. "Is it your first time on Martha's Vineyard?"

"It is," the man went on.

"I can't place your accent," Elsa said.

"I hail from Greece, originally," the man said.

"Oh! Greece. Wow." Carmella cupped her hands together. "And how are you enjoying our island?"

"It is gorgeous," the man said, his hand over his heart. "I'm exploring very slowly, taking many breaks for plenty of food and good wine."

"I think you're doing it right," Nancy heard herself say, surprising herself with how forthright she was.

"You three are from the island?"

"We are," Elsa said, gesturing toward Carmella.

"I'm from Brooklyn, originally," Nancy explained.

"Oh! But you came here to raise your daughters?" the Greek man asked.

Carmella and Elsa laughed gently.

"I'm not their real mother," Nancy explained. "I married their father, but he, unfortunately, passed away."

A shadow passed over the Greek man's face. "I am sorry to hear that. I do believe it's a wonderful thing that the three of you still laugh together like a family. I suppose you'll always be family."

"It is special," Elsa said thoughtfully.

"I count my blessings for my stepmother every day," Carmella said, drawing her hand over Nancy's on the table.

"What is your name?" Elsa asked.

"Kostos. And yours?"

They told him their names, with Nancy going last. She hated how thunderous her heartbeat sounded, as though her heart wanted to jump out of her body. Back in the old days, Nancy had prided herself on her bravery. She'd been as spontaneous as Alyssa but hadn't had very good instincts to go along with that, which had resulted in numerous mistakes. Falling in love with Neal had been a bit like walking into the ocean, feeling the water come up over her ankles, over her shins, until she'd been up to her shoulders in love— overwhelmed with it. She hadn't ever wanted to get out.

"I feel like it's up to us to show you around," Elsa said to Kostos. "As islanders, we can't just let you float around without rhyme or reason. What if you only see really touristy things? What if you go back to Greece without seeing what makes Martha's Vineyard really unique?"

"Terrifying," Carmella agreed.

Here, Kostos met Nancy's gaze with that same intensity. It was as though, already, through the air between their tables, they spoke to one another without the necessity of syllables or sounds. It was in this profound feeling of knowing someone, of being known, that Nancy heard herself speak.

"I'd love to show you around, Kostos."

Kostos studied her as Carmella and Elsa's eyes bugged out slightly, perhaps sensing the flirtation, the power of which existed somewhere above their heads.

"I'd like that very much," Kostos said, removing his phone from his pocket, trying to conceal his grin. "Now, what is it that they always say on American comedies? Can I have your digits?"

Carmella and Elsa cackled so that the table shook, the glasses of wine quivering.

"I take it nobody really says that?" Kostos' smile was enormous, handsome, and tremendously clever.

"You just did," Carmella quipped. "And I think it might have worked out in your favor."

Nancy's ears rang as she told him her number, watching as he typed it into his phone. All day, she'd sensed her life closing up, the avenues of possibility dying out. Yet here Kostos had been all along, waiting for her. Was it too good to be true?

Chapter Four

The cab from the Venice airport could only take them halfway to Teresa Cacciapaglia's villa. This stood to reason, as most of Venice's tremendous travel-ways were filled with water. Although Janine had read all about Venice, looked up photographs, and watched several films that took place there, nothing could fully prepare her for being there in real life. She was standing on the edge of a platform with her two girls, surrounded by their luggage, as a water taxi approached to pick them up. On both sides of the waterway were gorgeous buildings in ochre, dark green, and navy blue, just as fantastic looking as any painting. From a window across from her, a woman bent out and smashed a wooden block against a rug so that it puffed with dust.

"I can't believe we're here," Alyssa breathed, stepping out onto the water taxi, dragging her suitcase behind her. On the way, the suitcase kicked up between the water taxi and the dock, and Janine was frightened it would tumble into the water below. From the look on the water taxi employee's face, that sort of thing happened all the time.

He was bored by the idea of it. Still, before Maggie and Janine could bring their own bags across, he hurried forward to collect them, then ushered them onboard.

As it was morning, the water taxi was filled with commuters. Janine studied them as they crept down the water toward the villa. For nearly all of Janine's adult life, she hadn't had to worry about money, a fact dictated by her relationship with Jack. But before that, before Nancy had left New York City, Janine had known the weight and shape of poverty. She knew how tired it made you. She saw that fatigue echoed out on the faces of the commuters and tried to imagine where in the world they were off to. Didn't they know they lived in the most beautiful place in the world?

Then again, Janine lived in Martha's Vineyard and often had to remind herself of the beauty that surrounded her. Humans could get used to anything, which was both a tragedy and a wonderful thing.

After five stops along the water taxi route, Janine announced to her daughters it was time to get off. Both of them were bleary-eyed and exhausted after the flight, muttering about how uncomfortable they were. When Jack had been alive, they'd often flown on a private plane, and the girls had grown accustomed to traveling in such luxury. But after Alyssa had taken the plane in November of 2021 (which had resulted in a horrific incident with a Dutch guy she'd met through Cole), Janine had sold the plane, grateful not to deal with the moralistic questions that came with owning such a thing. Now that Maggie and Alyssa were a little bit older, both with babies on the way, they understood that much better than before.

Teresa's villa was located along the water, with a dramatic staircase that led to a large wooden door that, long ago, had been painted a deep red. Above the mailbox were tile letters that spelled out CACCIAPAGLIA. It seemed incredible to Janine that, all this time, Jack's mother had lived here, knowing of him, yet never reaching out to him. Jack hadn't bothered to come to see her, either.

What a waste.

"It looks haunted," Alyssa said, standing at the base of the steps and gazing up.

"No wonder Dad never wanted to come here," Maggie said. "He was always a scaredy-cat."

Janine laughed, shivering with nerves. It was funny to remember, so many years later, the fact that Jack never wanted to watch horror movies, that he often covered his eyes during action sequences. It was funny that a man who'd torn her heart to smithereens and then ultimately died of a heart attack could be frightened of such banal things.

Alyssa used the thick iron knocker to rap on the door, and a moment later, a dark-haired woman in her thirties answered. Janine had been told someone would be there, but it occurred to her she had no idea who this was. Family maybe?

"Hi," the woman said. "My name is Francesca. You must be Janine?"

Janine carried her suitcase up to stand next to Alyssa. "I'm Janine. These are my two daughters, Alyssa and Maggie."

"Pleasure to meet you." Francesca took first Alyssa's suitcase, then Janine's, then hurried down the steps to take Maggie's. "Until recently, I worked as Teresa's assistant. It's stated in her will that I continue to be paid six months after her death to ensure that everything is taken care of."

"Thank you," Janine said, studying how easily the woman jumped up and down the steps and then led them into the shadowed foyer, where immaculate and very old paintings and tapestries adorned the walls. It was looking more and more haunted by the second.

"The lawyer is already here," Francesca went on, snapping her hands together. "As you meet with him, I will take your bags to your rooms." She smiled serenely at first Alyssa, then Maggie, adding, "I know you never met your grandmother. She was a truly inspired woman. One of a kind. Unique, you might say."

Alyssa and Maggie exchanged curious glances.

"We're eager to learn more about her," Alyssa said.

"Oh. You will," Francesca said, then spun on her heel and led them into the adjoining dining room, where a very short man with a fat mustache sat in front of a thick folder. Francesca introduced them, then pulled out chairs for them to sit before the lawyer, whose name was Mario Benticcini.

As soon as Francesca was out of the room, Mario opened the folder, cleared his throat, and began to read.

"This is the last will and testament, by Teresa Cacciapaglia, which I have written in my own hand, in English— a language I have hardly spoken since I left the United States many, many years ago, especially given the fact that you, my dear and handsome son, have never visited."

Alyssa, Maggie, and Janine exchanged glances, sensing the volatility behind the woman's words.

"This isn't to say I'm angry with you, Jack," the lawyer went on. "Rather, as I studied you from a distance, with only the love a mother can offer her son, I recognized that you were never fully just your father. Rather, you were half mine, whimsical and alive and open to the mysticisms of the universe."

Janine felt like laughing, but she folded her lips and managed to keep it in. In truth: she'd fallen in love with Jack for these reasons, for his eagerness and his uniqueness, for his brash confidence, for everything he'd been. What he'd done in cheating on her didn't negate all that had come before that.

"In any case, Jack, now that you're here, in my home, so far from yours in Manhattan, it is time you play by my rules," the lawyer read.

"Rules?" Alyssa asked. "I don't understand."

The lawyer gave Alyssa a sharp look of disapproval. "The villa, all my belongings, and everything else I have to give will be yours, if and only if you play and win my game," the lawyer read.

"A game?" Maggie laughed and crossed her arms over her chest. "Now, this is starting to sound like a horror movie."

"Your first clue is this," the lawyer went on, clearly annoyed that they spoke over his performance. "Find me with the unburied woman who lost her son far too soon."

Alyssa and Maggie's jaws dropped.

"The unburied woman?" Alyssa demanded. "Is that really all you're giving us?"

"Once you discover the next clue, you will move on to the next, and the next, until all is revealed," the lawyer continued. "When you've discovered the truth and defeated the game, all my riches will be yours. Good luck to you, Jack. My condolences on the death of your mother."

Abruptly after he finished reading, the lawyer stood,

slid the first page of the will over to the three Potter women, packed up the rest of his things, and left. Alyssa, Maggie, and Janine sat in dumb silence, their heads spinning with jet lag, reading and rereading the letter.

"I seriously do not get it," Maggie said.

Footsteps outside the dining room made Janine leap from her chair. "Who's there?"

Francesca appeared in the doorway, laughing. "I'm sorry to scare you. This old house can give anyone a fright."

Janine grimaced and pointed to the will. "Have you read this?"

"She never let me, no." Francesca approached to read the letter, slowly smiling. In Italian, she said something nobody else understood, then mumbled, "I'm sorry. I was just thinking, what an incredible woman."

Alyssa laughed. "She was clearly unique, like you said."

"Any idea what this means?" Maggie asked.

Francesca scrunched up her face. "I don't know. I haven't eaten anything yet, and my brain just doesn't work when I haven't. Would any of you care for some croissants and espresso? I brought them in from a local bakery."

They couldn't refuse something like that. Francesca hurried into what was probably the kitchen, and, in a moment, there was the growling sound of the espresso machine.

"Francesca has to know something about this clue, right?" Alyssa said.

Maggie grumbled. "We're really going to play this weird game?" She glanced at Janine, adding, "I mean, isn't it a waste of time? Maybe we should just tell the lawyer to give the money to charity. We never knew her. For goodness' sake, Dad hardly knew her! And she clearly despised him for not having some kind of relationship with her."

"Where's your sense of adventure?" Alyssa demanded.

Janine winced. "Listen. You're both pregnant. If you want to take a few days to enjoy Venice, then fly home, that's fine with me."

"I really want to know Teresa's secrets," Alyssa said.

Francesca appeared with a platter of gorgeous croissants along with very tiny cups of espresso.

"That woman had plenty of secrets," Francesca said.

Alyssa looked mischievous. "Will you help us with the first clue?"

Francesca shifted her weight from foot to foot, clearly unsure.

"She's not here watching you," Janine offered.

Francesca laughed to herself. "I know that. I do. It's just that Teresa had a very particular way of living and now, of dying. I don't want to mess up her system."

"We just have no idea what it is," Alyssa explained. "We just got here. We don't know the city, and we—"

"Find me with the unburied woman who lost her son far too soon," Maggie interrupted, reading the will again. "Does that mean anything to you?"

Francesca's lips quivered into a smile. "Well, the Cacciapaglias have an enormous section of the cemetery near here. They are an incredibly noble family. It was a good bit of luck, being hired to work for them."

"Are there any unburied women there?" Maggie asked, shivering, even though it was clear she wanted to tell a joke.

But at this, Alyssa jumped from her chair to grab a croissant. "Italians often bury their dead in mausoleums. Isn't that right, Francesca?"

"It is, indeed," Francesca said. "It's where your grandmother was buried, after all. In a mausoleum her father purchased for her before she turned ten years old. In Italy, our culture is tremendously old— and we must face death in a different way than Americans."

Over the table, Janine, Alyssa, and Maggie exchanged glances, alternating between feeling freaked out and excited. Finally, Janine shrugged and said, "We should pay your grandmother a visit, anyway. Don't you think?"

Chapter Five

Around noon, Nancy got her first call from her girls in Venice. She answered it while seated on the back porch of the big, empty Remington House, her heart in her throat. A live video appeared on the screen of her phone, one that seemed impossible in its beauty. There Janine, Alyssa, and Maggie stood on a gorgeous bridge overlooking a canal in Venice. A gondola floated past, complete with an Italian rower onboard. If Nancy wasn't mistaken, she thought she could hear him singing.

"Hi, Grandma! Buongiorno!" Alyssa cried.

Nancy laughed and placed her hand over her chest. "Goodness. You three look beautiful. What time is it there?"

"Six in the evening," Janine explained. "We arrived at the villa earlier this afternoon and met with Teresa's lawyer, which was..."

"Interesting, to say the least," Maggie finished her mother's sentence.

"Interesting how?"

Summer Rush

Janine went on to explain Teresa's "game," along with their plans to head to the mausoleum tomorrow to investigate.

"But we decided we wanted to settle in today, go out to eat, and explore the city a bit," Janine finished.

Nancy shook her head. Death was such a messy, complicated, heartbreaking thing. It boggled her mind that Teresa had wanted to make a game of hers. Then again, perhaps she'd been mostly alone during her old age. Perhaps this had allowed her space and time to concoct ideas like this.

On top of that, Nancy had a hunch Teresa had been resentful of Jack and his refusal to ever know her. Perhaps, had Janine never returned to Nancy's life, Nancy would have felt the same way.

But despite Nancy and Janine's closeness, when Janine asked Nancy what she was up to, Nancy heard herself tell a lie of omission.

"Not up to much. I'm going to do a bit of gardening later, then head up to the Lodge to teach two yoga classes, back-to-back. I'll probably go to bed early tonight."

Even as she said it, her stomach curdled. But she managed to get through the rest of the phone call before she keeled over on the back porch and stared at her shoes, gasping for breath.

"*Pull yourself together, Nancy. You're an old woman going on a date. You've been on hundreds of dates before.*" Hundreds, of course, was probably an over-exaggeration. Still, back in her teens, twenties, and thirties, there had been many men— all of them egotistical, ready to take her for all she was worth emotionally. "You aren't that person anymore," Nancy continued to whisper to herself. "You've grown so much! Act like it."

Kostos had invited her out to dinner that night. Over text, shivering like a frightened rabbit, Nancy had suggested they meet downtown early so that she could give him a short tour of historic Edgartown. He'd agreed wholeheartedly.

Nancy donned an ochre jumpsuit with long, flowing pants and a top that was cut like a sharp square over her upper chest. Although she was in her sixties, she'd been committed to yoga for so many years that she felt confident showing her arms. Even still, the mirror showed loose skin, which caught the light that streamed in through her bedroom windows. She wouldn't have told anyone in the world that the loose skin bothered her. But it did.

At six-thirty sharp, Nancy strode along the Edgartown boardwalk, scanning for Kostos— that hunky man who made her heart flip over in a way that made her feel like a teenager again. Just when she thought that maybe, he'd stood her up, that maybe, he didn't have time for her after all, she spotted him leaning against the boardwalk railing with his eyes toward the lighthouse. He wore a white button-down and a pair of dark jeans, and his hands were clasped together, his eyes heavy with thought.

For a little while, Nancy wasn't sure what to do. Interrupting him seemed like a tragedy, as he seemed like the kind of man who could spontaneously write a poem, just in his head, as he looked at something as stunning as the late afternoon on Martha's Vineyard.

But before she could decide what to do or what to say to bring him back to earth, Kostos flinched as though he'd realized she was near, turned toward her, and smiled. This time, it was Nancy's turn to float off the planet.

"Nancy!" Kostos strode toward her, opening his arms,

then kissed her on both cheeks— as Nancy had seen Italians and French people do. It was bizarre, as an American, to be greeted like this, but Nancy decided to roll with it. It had been ages since a man's lips had been so close to hers.

After a brief tour downtown, during which Kostos asked numerous questions about the history of the island, he finally admitted he was "so hungry" that he couldn't possibly concentrate on anything else until he ate. Nancy laughed, remembering that Neal had been similar when it had come to food.

Nancy had made reservations at a fish restaurant that served the catch of the day with delectable sides, like buttery asparagus or garlic mashed potatoes, plus homemade bread with butter that tasted like a cloud. They sat at a table on the front porch with a pretty good view of the harbor, where the sailboats creaked against the docks, prepared for their next outings. Kostos knew a great deal about the wine on the menu, and Nancy let him take charge, asking questions about the grapes and vineyards he didn't know well. The server was happy to share his knowledge, even slightly arrogant about it. After Kostos opted for an orange chardonnay, the server left them, and Kostos winked at Nancy, saying, "They love showing off what they know. I understand that well. I worked in the service industry for years."

"Did you?" Nancy tilted her head. "I had a few stints in restaurants, as well. But I never knew as much about wine as you seem to."

"I worked at a luxury restaurant in Greece," Kostos explained. "It was essential to impress the clientele with the very best wine knowledge. Every region in Italy,

Greece, France, Germany, Austria, and on and on. California was a part of the equation, too, of course."

"That sounds intimidating."

Kostos laughed. "It was. But I learned a thing or two about hanging out with that kind of crowd. I didn't come from money, and all the money I have is hard-earned. But the rich folks I met at the restaurant taught me to walk the walk and talk the talk, which is essential if you want to sell yourself."

"I understand that. I came from nothing, absolutely nothing. But after I married my late husband, I found myself in a very different world. I recently watched the film *Pretty Woman* and realized I had a lot in common with Julia Roberts' character, at least back then. I was a mess."

"I'm sure you weren't," Kostos said. "From here, you seem like a remarkable, well-dressed, beautiful, and elegant woman. I can't imagine you not knowing which side of the plate the forks go."

"And in which order the forks are meant to go," Nancy added. "Trust me. I checked out plenty of books from the library on that very subject. It was important for me to show off for Neal, at least for a little while."

Kostos shook his head. "Isn't it funny, the things we humans get bogged down by?"

"I know! A fork is a fork," Nancy said with a laugh. "Until it's not."

The server returned with their wine and took their food orders, Nancy with the sea bass and Kostos with the salmon. Nancy found herself continually drawn to his eyes, falling into that blue ocean.

"By the way," Kostos said, his face earnest. "I hope

this doesn't sound bizarre or out of bounds. But I wanted to say I lost my wife, too. A few years ago."

"Oh. I'm so sorry."

"I'm sorry about your loss, too." Kostos palmed the back of his neck. "It doesn't really get any easier, I guess. But I've found ways to carry it.

Nancy nodded, knowing exactly what he meant. She sipped her wine and stumbled through her thoughts, feeling inarticulate. And then, perhaps because she hadn't spoken to anyone about it since she'd found out, she heard herself say, "I recently learned that my husband wasn't entirely kind to his first wife."

"That sounds complicated," Kostos offered.

"Yeah. My stepdaughter discovered a diary from her mother, my husband's first wife. It sounds like he was quite cruel to her. He pushed her to have an affair. She nearly left him."

"Why didn't she?" Kostos asked.

"The man she was having an affair with died in a tragic accident," Nancy said. "And she had two young children at home. She was reeling with grief, and I don't think she wanted to do life by herself. Not then."

Kostos' face was shadowed with sorrow. "That's a terrible story."

"It's been hard for me to reconcile the Neal I knew with the one from the diaries," Nancy offered.

"Did he ever treat you the way he treated his first wife?"

Nancy shook her head. "Never. He always made me feel very loved, very respected. He completely changed my life."

Kostos raised his shoulders. "It sounds like he

changed. That, or you were just better suited to one another. Or a mix of both."

Nancy blinked back tears. She hadn't expected such compassion from a stranger.

"I'm sure if you'd met me when I was a younger man, you would have thought I was very arrogant," Kostos continued, his grin crooked.

"Would I?" Nancy crossed her arms over her chest. Was she flirting?

"I can almost guarantee it," Kostos said.

The server came soon with their dinner, and Nancy fell quiet, listening to the rushing ocean along the docks, the conversation of the couples around them, and the soft scrape of Kostos' fork and knife against his plate. When she raised her eyes to look at him, she caught his, and they held one another's gaze for a long moment. It felt like magic.

After dinner, Kostos and Nancy walked along the boardwalk, their hands swinging very close to one another. Nancy was telling him about how big and empty her house felt, especially now that her girls were in Venice.

"Oh, I just love Venice." Kostos stopped walking for a moment as though the memory of that city had taken him outside of himself.

"They seem to love it," Nancy said. "My daughter's mother-in-law is from there, but she recently passed away and left everything to my grandchildren, Alyssa and Maggie. But apparently, it's not as simple as that. She's set up some sort of scavenger hunt. If they win the hunt, they get what's theirs."

"And if they don't?" Kostos asked.

Nancy shrugged. "I don't know!"

"It sounds like something from a film," Kostos offered.

Nancy laughed. "It's bizarre, isn't it? But my granddaughters are both about to have babies, and I think it's a nice distraction before everything changes forever."

Kostos' eyes twinkled. "You're going to be a great-grandmother?"

Nancy's cheeks burned. "I didn't even think about that. That sounds ancient, doesn't it?"

"It sounds like a blessing," Kostos corrected her, finally taking her hand in his. "It sounds like a brilliant next era of your life."

Nearly swooning, Nancy breathed deeply, knowing he was right.

Chapter Six

Jet lag kept Alyssa, Maggie, and Janine in bed far too late. Janine burst up around one in the afternoon the day after their arrival, groggy, her hair in a wild mess, then slowly made her way to the window to peer out at the canal below. Italy had awoken many, many hours ago. People were going to lunch.

"Girls! Hello!" Janine knocked on first Alyssa's bedroom door, then Maggie's, before she opened Alyssa's and peered in. The thick, black curtains drawn over the windows brought in no light, and the room was cool and comfortable. According to Francesca, the rooms they slept in had all been used as guest bedrooms during Teresa's life there, as she hadn't had children outside of Jack. Nobody had dared go into Teresa's bedroom yet, perhaps due to fear of her, of where she'd died. Or perhaps out of respect.

"Mom?" Alyssa groaned and stretched her arms over her head. "What time is it?"

"You don't want to know," Janine said with a laugh.

Suddenly, Maggie's bedroom door burst open, and

Maggie stumbled into the hallway, rubbing her eyes, just as she'd done when she'd been a child. "I could not get to sleep until really late," she said. "And just when I started to, the baby woke me up."

"I had the same problem!" Alyssa cried. "What is up with your baby, Maggie? She or he hates me."

Maggie rolled her eyes, laughing as Alyssa joined them in the hallway. It was true, of course, that Alyssa was carrying Maggie and Rex's baby— that she'd offered when Maggie couldn't get pregnant. Maggie's pregnancy a couple of months later had come as a thunderous surprise.

Janine hadn't asked the girls their plans for after they delivered. She assumed Alyssa would want to be a part of the babies' lives and would want to help raise them. But in truth, both babies were Maggie's— and Maggie, being Maggie, would want the most control over the children.

Downstairs, they found a note from Francesca on the table. In it, she explained how to work the espresso machine and that she'd brought more croissants. Beneath that, she'd written the address of the cemetery where Teresa had been buried.

"Good luck on your scavenger hunt," she finished.

At the breakfast table, Maggie and Alyssa sipped tea as Janine made herself an espresso and passed out the croissants. When she opened the kitchen curtains, the light was blistering, so she closed them again shortly thereafter. She wasn't sure how they would make it to the cemetery that day.

But by the time four rolled around, they began to kick into gear. Showered, dressed in summer dresses and sandals, they left the villa and headed straight for the nearest water taxi station. As the boat floated toward them, laden with a mix of tourists and locals, Janine turned back to gaze up at the villa. It seemed impossible that it served as their current "home," although right now, they accepted it easily, sliding into their Italian lives.

The Venice cemetery was situated on the island of San Michele and was the final resting place of several famous people— composers, poets, and even physicists. Tourists stood outside the gates, along the steps, listening to a tour guide who spoke very quick Polish as Janine, Alyssa, and Maggie walked up toward the entrance, captivated by the spooky, old-world beauty.

The Cacciapaglia mausoleum was located toward the back of the cemetery, between two tall cypress trees. Inside the mausoleum was a dramatic statue of the Virgin Mary, her hand over her chest, and beneath her were offerings of flowers and candles. Janine breathed slowly, studying the other Cacciapaglias who'd died long before.

"Wow. The first person was buried here in 1493?" Alyssa pointed to the aged tile.

Not long after they entered, they found Teresa's name, along with her birth and death date. The death date had been newly carved and played in sharp contrast to the rest of the mausoleum. Maggie reached out to touch the etching, her eyes shining.

"It's so strange that we never knew her," she offered.

"It's not our fault," Alyssa tried. "But I know what you mean."

After another long, heavy moment of silence, Alyssa said, "Remember the clue. 'The unburied woman who lost her son far too soon.'"

Maggie winced. "I don't like to say this. But it must be referring to a child?"

Janine scanned the names, the birth and death dates,

trying to feel the immensity of all these lives. "Oh! What about him?" She hurried across the mausoleum toward a tile that read: Tristram Cacciapaglia: April 2, 1991- April 29, 1991.

"Oh no." Maggie dropped her gaze. "I just hate that."

Alyssa joined Janine near the tile, frowning. "Teresa must have meant this baby, right? And..." She pointed to the tile directly next to it, upon which had been written: Eva Cacciapaglia: June 19, 1971. "Eva hasn't died yet!"

Janine stuttered. "What do you mean?" She'd assumed they would find a clue from Teresa at the mausoleum itself, however impossible that sounded.

"The unburied woman! Eva hasn't died yet. She hasn't been buried! And Tristram was her son!" Alyssa said.

"My gosh." Maggie shook her head, impressed.

"We have to find her," Alyssa insisted.

"But how do we get a hold of her?" Maggie asked.

Alyssa thought for a moment, then removed her phone from her purse and typed and typed and typed. "I found her social media!"

Janine and Maggie's jaws dropped. Social media was the strangest thing to consider, especially from within the walls of a mausoleum. But Alyssa was right: Eva wasn't dead. She had a life, a social network. She was reachable through modern means.

Alyssa typed out a message that she asked Janine and Maggie's approval of:

Dear Eva. You don't know me, but my name is Alyssa Potter, and my biological grandmother was Teresa Cacciapaglia, your relative. I am very sorry for your recent loss. It's a tragedy that I never knew her. In any case, I'm in the city, and I wondered if you wanted to meet up. I would love to talk to you about something Teresa said in her will. All the best, Alyssa.

* * *

Immediately after Alyssa pressed send on her social media message, Janine, Maggie, and Alyssa stared intently at her phone, there in the mausoleum, waiting. It was an incredibly anticlimactic moment, interrupted only by a stream of tourists in the cemetery, talking a little too loudly, given the environment.

"Let's get out of here," Alyssa said with a sigh. "If she writes me back, she writes me back. If she doesn't..."

"We'll find her another way," Janine assured her. "She's the next clue. She has to be."

Janine suggested they head back to the area of Venice nearest the villa, where they could grab a snack and think about what to do next. Although Alyssa was clearly disappointed, stuck in a wild goose chase, she reluctantly agreed, and together, the three Potter women disembarked on a water taxi, away from the mausoleum where so many relatives they would never know were buried.

At a little café in a piazza near the villa, they ordered mini pizzas, focaccia, and a plate of cheese, with Janine opting for an Aperol Spritz, which gleamed like an orange in the sun. Both Alyssa and Maggie ordered mock-cocktails that imitated margaritas, which Maggie wrinkled her nose at upon drinking. "This thing is ninety-nine percent sugar!"

Alyssa cackled. "That's why it's good!"

Maggie folded her lips, clearly ready to change the subject— and avoid her virgin margarita. "What did you see on Eva's social media? Anything interesting?"

Alyssa brought back up the social media page, which showed a woman in her fifties with jet-black hair and an iconic smile not unlike Teresa's.

"What relation is she to Teresa?" Janine asked.

Alyssa scanned through a "family members" section of Eva's page, but unfortunately, Teresa wasn't listed.

"Given her age, I'm guessing she was a niece?" Maggie said.

"Not a bad guess," Janine offered. "Was she ever married?"

"I don't think so," Alyssa said, "which means she had her baby out of wedlock. Wouldn't that have been a pretty big scandal here in Italy back then?"

Janine nodded, a wave of sorrow flowing through her. "It's not that the United States doesn't have its own problems around shaming young women," she began, "but I think in Italy, it was that much worse. Misogyny was and still is a huge problem."

Alyssa and Maggie were quiet for a few moments, eyeing one another.

"I feel frightened, sometimes, about bringing a little girl into the world," Maggie admitted. "Things have gotten so much better for us, but..."

"But there's still work to do," Alyssa affirmed. "And it's up to us to do that."

Janine's heart swelled with pride for her girls. "You really don't want to learn the sex?"

Alyssa and Maggie shook their heads, flashing gleeful smiles.

"I want it to be a surprise," Maggie said.

"And Maggie gets what she wants," Alyssa said. "She's the mother, after all."

There was a ding from Alyssa's phone, and the three of them bent down with excitement to read:

Alyssa! Wonderful of you to reach out. Yes, we must meet. How long are you in Venice? Would you like to come to my home in two nights' time? I will make you my mother's recipe. (P.s. My mother was Teresa's sister. I suppose that makes us cousins, of a sort.)

"I guess that answers that question," Alyssa said. "You up for dinner with Eva?"

Maggie and Janine nodded exuberantly.

"I'll do anything for that family recipe," Janine offered. "All your grandmother passed to me was how to make Hot Pockets in the microwave."

Alyssa and Maggie laughed gently, with Maggie adding, "Is that why you tried to pass on so many recipes to us?"

"They made it to you, Mags," Alyssa joked. "I have a long way to go in the kitchen."

Eva's home was located along a canal a few waterways from Teresa's villa. It was not difficult to imagine Teresa and Eva visiting one another, perhaps on the very water taxi the three of them now sat upon. Although it was still August, clouds rolled over the water-logged city, and, frequently, rain pattered across the canals, giving the city an eerie feeling. Janine eyed Maggie, then Alyssa, her heart jumping nervously. What on earth would Eva tell them about Teresa? And how long would they play along with Teresa's game until they decided to go home?

Still, Janine couldn't help but be excited, caught up in this adventure with her daughters.

The woman who opened the front door of the canalside home did, in fact, look a great deal like Teresa. Although her hair was graying around her ears and crown, it was still sleek and thick, and she looked strong and agile despite her fifty-something years. When she first locked eyes on them, her face erupted with joy, and she leaped forward with hugs, kisses, and "buongiornos" until Janine's cheeks burned with a mix of embarrassment and confusion. In the United States, people were friendly— but this was another level.

"I'm sorry," Eva said, opening the door wider to let them in. "I loved my Aunt Teresa so, so dearly, and to have you three here in the wake of her death means a great deal."

Alyssa, Maggie, and Janine followed Eva through the shadowed hallways toward a living room located on the opposite side of the house. Eva had hung beautiful, modern paintings that contrasted the antique feel of the rest of the city, and there was a liveliness to the furniture — a bright red couch, a navy chaise longue, a monstera plant. It was clear she was the kind of woman who never wanted to grow old.

"Please! Sit," Eva instructed before disappearing to fetch cannoli and espresso. When she reappeared in the living room, she eyed Alyssa, then Maggie, and laughed. "You two will not take the espresso."

"Unfortunately not," Alyssa said. "We can drink small amounts of coffee, but..."

"But this is too much." Eva placed the espresso cups and the cannoli on the coffee table, then hurried away to grab glasses of water instead. When she returned, she sat between Alyssa and Maggie and took their hands. "Both of you! Pregnant. Why did you not tell me?"

"It's an awkward thing to bring up over text," Alyssa said with a laugh.

Maggie blushed yet smiled in a secretive way. Janine

knew that Maggie loved to talk about her pregnancy, about the expectation of tomorrow. Every time someone brought it up, she glowed.

"When are you due?" Eva asked.

"I'm in November, and Maggie's in January," Alyssa responded.

"Wonderful. Just wonderful." Eva locked eyes with Janine, then added, "Mother must be very pleased?"

"Very pleased, yes," Janine said, smiling.

"I truly wish Teresa could have known you," Eva said, nodding first to Janine, then to Alyssa and Maggie. "She didn't speak often of her son, Jack, but I know she felt a great deal of love and, of course, loss." Eva swallowed, clearly thinking about her own son, who'd died so long ago. Janine wondered why Eva had never tried to have another child. Perhaps the pain had been too great.

Despite all Janine had lost, she'd never gone through something like that.

"Will you tell us more about her?" Alyssa asked.

"She was an incredible woman. An intellectual. A mystic. She had this way about her, of knowing what was going to happen next, which often terrified the rest of the family. For a little while, she ran a psychic service, and women from all over Italy came to her villa to learn about their fate or about how to avoid a fate she felt sure was coming for them.

"I know what you're thinking," Eva went on. "That she was a hack. That she made it all up. But I had enough experiences with her to recognize her incredible gifts." Eva closed her eyes for a moment, taking short, clipped breaths. "Because you're here, I suppose you know a large part of my story. When I was young, I gave birth to a little boy, who died a month later. After he died, I went to

Aunt Teresa's, and I asked her what I should do. How can I get through this horrific pain? And the things she told me, which I will not mention here, ultimately saved my life."

Eva's eyes were wistful, caught up in the past. Alyssa was captivated by her, while Maggie seemed more doubtful. Janine wasn't sure where she stood.

"But even more than all that, she had a wicked sense of humor. She was a completely unique individual, someone I admired. When I was younger, I thought my mother was boring, stuck-up, but Aunt Teresa was always running with the wind, it seemed to me. When I was very young, she ran off with that American man, your grandfather." Eva's eyes met Janine's for a moment as she added, "I can't imagine what it must have been like to marry into a family like that. I suppose you know better than most."

Janine's throat was tight. Meekly, she said, "I felt like Cinderella at the ball for a little while."

"I think Aunt Teresa did, too. Of course, she was never one to be taken advantage of, and she took the next plane she could when she learned of her husband's affair." Eva's eyes were shadowed, and she folded her hands on her lap.

"It's been strange, being here," Janine finally offered. "Seeing the world that Jack never got to see. Sleeping in his mother's house."

Eva grimaced. "His death was tragic. He was much too young."

Alyssa and Maggie stared at the floor.

"But Teresa never knew about it?" Janine asked.

Eva shook her head. "She was very sick the past few years. She saw very few people."

"I assume she saw you?" Janine asked.

"She did, but not always," Eva added tentatively. "It completely depended on her mood. I suppose, in that way, I already started to mourn her, even when she was still living just a few streets away."

Alyssa squeezed Eva's hand, and her eyes were moist, the tears threatening to spill.

"Oh, but we're all here together now," Eva said, sniffing. "I can't believe it, really. When Teresa told me she wanted me to play a part in her little game, I said, 'You really think these Americans are going to come all the way here? You must be mad!' But she looked at me with that twinkle in her eye and said, 'You wait. They'll come.' I should have known she was right."

Eva stood and walked regally to the bookshelf, where she removed an entire shelf's worth of books. One after another, she piled them on the table beside the shelf as Janine, Maggie, and Alyssa watched, captivated. When the books were cleared, Eva turned and gave them a secretive smile.

"It's very old, you see. I can't risk it being in too much sunlight." She then opened what looked like a trapdoor behind where the books had been and procured a very thick leather book. It looked to weigh nearly twenty pounds.

"What is that?" Alyssa stood and walked toward her, mesmerized.

"Careful," Eva said. "I'm going to find something to wrap it up safely in." She placed the book delicately in Alyssa's arms as though it was as precious as a baby and then hustled off to the next room.

When Alyssa turned with the book in her arms, she caught Janine's eye. "What the heck is this?"

Janine shook her head. "What's it called?"

Alyssa's tone was overtly American. "The title is, *La Nascita del Rinascimento e Dopo.*"

Maggie chuckled into her hand. "Nice Italian accent, sis."

"Is that the clue?" Janine asked.

Alyssa shrugged and turned as Eva came back. "What are we supposed to do with this?"

Eva laughed. "Teresa didn't tell me! She just said to give you this book when you came to my door."

Janine dropped back on the couch, at a loss. "We can't speak Italian."

"I don't know if she considered that," Eva said.

"Maybe you could help us?" Alyssa suggested.

"I don't know." Eva flipped through the first several pages, scanning quickly. "It seems like a very old book about art. Nothing about it stands out to me as a clue."

"Is anything underlined?" Maggie asked.

"Not that I can see," Eva said, frowning. "Listen, girls. I had better get started on my mother's pasta sauce. If I don't do it correctly, I can hear her screaming at me. She's been deceased for five years, and still, she has this power!"

Using the canvas bags Eva gave them, Janine and Maggie wrapped up the book, listening as Alyssa and Eva gossiped in the kitchen.

"Alyssa is really into this," Maggie said thoughtfully.

"You're not?"

"It's not that it's not interesting," Maggie offered. "It's just strange. This woman laid out all these clues for us. Where is this headed? I don't trust it."

When Alyssa and Maggie had been little girls, it had always been this way. Although she was younger, Alyssa had always been the first to climb to the top of the monkey bars, always the first to race the boys. Maggie had always sat back, watching, thinking.

"Like I said before. It's just a vacation. And we're meeting a distant relative of yours! Isn't that incredible? I mean, when the babies get a little bit older, you'll be able to bring them here, to show them the villa, and to introduce them to Eva."

Maggie's lips curled into a smile. Always, it was easy to cheer her up, talking about the future— about the babies yet to be born. With the book secure in its packaging, Janine rubbed Maggie's shoulder, then tilted her head toward the kitchen. "Why don't we join them? I can't believe it because it seems like we just ate, but I'm already starving."

"Sounds like you're half-Italian, already," Maggie said with a laugh.

"No, honey. You're Italian," Janine reminded her. "I'm just along for the ride."

Chapter Seven

After their luxurious meal at Eva's, Janine, Maggie, and Alyssa chatted with Eva for a long while, about her life in Italy, about her friends and the rest of the Cacciapaglia family, and about her recommendations for the remainder of their stay in Venice.

"We don't know when we're going back," Alyssa explained, then placed her hand across her stomach. "We're at the mercy of Teresa's game now."

Eva laughed openly, waving her hand. "I can't imagine it'll take you longer than a week or two."

"Have you seen that book?" Alyssa asked again, gesturing toward the enormous, old-world book that served as their next clue. "It'll take us a lifetime to go through it."

"I imagine Teresa knew Jack couldn't speak Italian," Eva said thoughtfully. "He never had any reason to learn it, did he?"

Janine shook her head. Jack had never considered learning another language, not that she knew of, anyway.

Perhaps, during his affair with Maxine, he'd spoken a bit of French. As this thought floated in and out of her mind, she waited for the pain which so often accompanied any thought of Maxine and Jack together. To her surprise, the pain didn't come. She felt almost as though they were people she'd met in another life.

"What I mean is, Teresa must have decided to use that book for reasons that extend beyond language," Eva suggested. "I wouldn't begin by translating the entire tome. Rather, think outside the box, if you can."

After they kissed Eva on both cheeks and bid her goodbye, Janine, Alyssa, and Maggie stepped back into the blissful night, where a moon hung low, casting a shimmering light across the canals. On the water taxi back to Teresa's villa, Alyssa clung hard to the large book, her eyes to the water, as Maggie texted her boyfriend, David, furiously.

"How is David doing?" Janine asked.

Maggie glanced up, jolting out of her phone-world. "He's okay. He and his mother worked at the bookstore today. He had a signing, and it sounds like it brought in quite a few new customers."

"That's wonderful," Janine said. "Did I tell you I finished reading *The Lighthouse on Arkin Bay*?"

Maggie's eyes lit up. "I forgot to ask you about that! What did you think?"

"David is a sensational writer," Janine said. "Although I have to admit, I was terrified for at least fifty percent of the book."

Alyssa perked up, intrigued. "Does his writing ever come through his personality? Like, does he ever creep you out?"

Maggie giggled. "No! His books and his personality

couldn't be more different. That, or he works out all of his complicated emotions within the books."

"That makes sense," Janine offered. "I had a few writing friends in the city, and they all said that thriller writers were the kindest writers of them all."

"Maybe everyone should write thrillers," Alyssa suggested.

"Maybe that's what Teresa set out to do with this scavenger hunt," Janine said.

Alyssa's eyes widened. "You're right! It's like the early start of a thriller."

Maggie shifted on her water taxi bench. "I don't like the sound of that."

"You'll have to ask David what happens next in a story like this," Alyssa said, swatting Maggie on the shoulder. "Please!"

Maggie grimaced and retreated into her phone, texting out the question. "I don't think I'm going to like what he says."

A full minute later, David texted back with the following:

> Hmm. What happens next in this story? Maybe someone also knows about the scavenger hunt— and follows you to steal the treasure!

Maggie shrieked as she read the text aloud, then glanced around the water taxi. "You haven't noticed anyone following us, have you?"

Both Janine and Alyssa laughed.

"Maggie, David just made that up!" Alyssa pointed out. "Nothing like that is going to happen."

Maggie folded her lips. "I shouldn't have asked him.

The thought alone is giving me the creeps. That, and the weird book Eva gave us. That thing is obviously possessed or something."

Back in the villa, Janine made them cups of tea and then opened the large, water-logged art book, bending over it to analyze the very small font, the miles and miles of text, discussing the intricate differences between various eras of art over the past five centuries. The clock on the wall read nine, then ten, then ten-thirty, and still, it seemed that they parsed through nothing of meaning with no clues in sight.

"Eva said to think outside the box," Alyssa said, rubbing her eyes.

"But I don't think I can think at all anymore," Maggie said. "Maybe we should go to sleep and try again tomorrow?" She paused, sipped her cold tea, and eyed Janine nervously. "We've been locking the door at night, haven't we?"

"Of course, honey." Janine placed her hand over Maggie's on the table, touched that Maggie was frightened and wanted to lean on her mother for safety. "What David told you was completely fictional. You heard what Eva said earlier. Venice is one of the safest places in all of Italy. You can sleep peacefully."

* * *

Up in her bedroom, Janine sat in shorts and an oversized t-shirt and called Henry, whom she'd begun to miss terribly. It was just past five on the east coast of the United States, and Henry was hard at work in his studio, cutting and editing and re-editing another documentary. Often, when he fell so deeply into his work, he edited all evening and into the morning— forgetting to take breaks and driving himself insane. This was another reason, Janine knew, that they should move in together soon. He needed someone to reel him in, to tell him to rest.

"How is it?" Henry asked, sounding slightly outside of himself.

Janine explained what had happened in the mausoleum and at Eva's home, and Henry was fascinated, asking numerous questions about the cemetery, Eva's house, Eva's relationship with Teresa, and how much Eva knew about the scavenger hunt.

"It sounds like this woman has a lot of mischief up her sleeves," Henry said.

"I can tell you want to do a documentary about this." Janine giggled.

"Is it so obvious? I mean, Alyssa and Maggie are learning about their family in real time through an intricate puzzle game. This stuff doesn't happen outside the movies," Henry said.

"David thinks it's like a thriller," Janine said.

Henry cackled. "David's a writer. He can't turn his storytelling brain off."

"And I think it's driving Maggie up the wall," Janine said.

Throughout the rest of the call, Henry spoke tenderly about the island, about the long hike he'd gone on last night, and about the dinner he planned to cook for a friend tomorrow. Slowly, he lulled Janine into a sleepy and soft mood, and after they said they loved one another, she hung up, tucked herself between the covers, and fell into a deep, dreamless sleep.

When Janine awoke the following morning, she padded downstairs to find Alyssa already up. She'd brewed a big pot of tea and had even run down the street to get baked goods, which now sat on a plate in the center of the kitchen table.

"And I got a big bag of lemons at the market!" Alyssa said, smiling proudly as she pointed at them. "I thought we could make fresh lemonade later."

In front of Alyssa sat the enormous Italian art book, wide open, with Alyssa's finger drawing line after line as she skimmed through.

"When did you get to work on that?" Janine asked, heading for the espresso machine.

"I couldn't sleep very well," Alyssa admitted. "It was like the book was calling to me."

Janine laughed. "Has it said anything else?"

"Well..."

At the espresso machine, Janine spun on her heel and stared at her daughter. "You found a clue?"

Alyssa raised her shoulders. "I think I'm beginning to understand why Teresa gave it to us."

Suddenly, Maggie appeared in the doorway to the kitchen, groggy and yawning herself out of slumber. "You're still reading through that heinous book?"

Alyssa waved Maggie and Janine toward her, shimmering with pride. "I realized that toward the middle of the book are several tiny, tiny cut-outs."

"Cut outs?" Maggie frowned.

Alyssa swept through the pages until, sure enough, she pointed at a tiny square cut-out, which had removed a single letter from a word. The cut was very precise, as though Teresa had used a very sharp, very small knife—perhaps an exacto.

"I've been looking up the words," Alyssa explained, "to see which letters are left out. And on this piece of paper, I've been writing out the letters to see if they form some kind of word."

Already, Alyssa had written down: s, s, o, and t.

"Toss," Maggie said with a shrug.

"I don't know how many letters she cut out," Alyssa said. "It takes a while, skimming through the book to make sure I haven't missed any. After that, I'm assuming we'll have to reorder the letters to make a word."

"And I'm sure that word will be in Italian," Janine said, wrinkling her nose.

"Maybe Eva can help us with that part," Maggie suggested, dropping into the kitchen chair beside Alyssa and taking a pastry. "Why don't we trade off on searching for cut-outs? You have a crazy look in your eyes, Alyssa. I think you need a break."

Throughout the rest of that morning, Janine, Maggie, and Alyssa traded off time slots with the book, scouring the lines for cut-outs and scribing any missing letters. By lunch, they were starving, and they allowed themselves a multi-course meal in the sun before they returned to work diligently in the kitchen of the villa. By nightfall, they'd collected five more letters, and by afternoon of the following day, they'd collected enough to sense they had something of meaning, something they could show to Eva.

But before they could invite Eva over, there was a knock at the front door. It was Francesca, Teresa's secretary.

"Oh! Wonderful," Alyssa said, hurrying from the door. "We need your help."

Francesca followed Alyssa into the kitchen, where she smiled prettily at Maggie and Janine. Janine felt as though they'd gone slightly manic, obsessing over the book and its little cut-outs for more than twenty-four hours at this point.

"We have these fifteen letters," Alyssa said proudly, showing off the scramble of letters on the notepad. "And we're pretty sure they form an Italian word or phrase, one that will be useful for us for our next clue."

"Oh! Which clue number is this?" Francesca asked.

"Technically, it's our second," Maggie said.

"So, the mausoleum had answers?" Francesca removed a pair of reading glasses from her purse and slid them up her nose.

"That led us to our long-lost cousin, Eva," Alyssa explained.

"Oh, wonderful. Teresa always adored Eva," Francesca said.

"She's lovely," Janine agreed.

For a long time, Francesca analyzed the list of letters, her eyes twitching as they went back and forth over the notepad. Maggie, Janine, and Alyssa remained very quiet and respectful as Janine stirred in doubt about the quest in the first place. Maybe the cut-out letters had been a coincidence, left over from an original owner of the book?

Finally, Francesca's smile erupted, and she said, "Ah! Of course. It's Paradiso Terrestre."

Alyssa clapped her hands. "Paradiso Terrestre! What is that?"

Francesca placed the notepad back on the kitchen table, her mental energy spent. "It's a painting. A very famous Italian painting. And it's housed in a museum in Venice, in fact."

"Really!" Alyssa turned to stare at Maggie, then Janine. Janine's heartbeat escalated. This really was beginning to feel like a thriller.

"Yes. It's in the Gallerie dell'Accademia," Francesca explained.

"We can't just take a painting out of a museum," Maggie said. "So, I don't know exactly what Teresa means by this?"

"It's the only clue we have," Alyssa said. "We have to go to the museum and see what happens next. Teresa's plan is in place, and we're just along for the ride."

Chapter Eight

Nancy finished her yoga class at seven in the morning, then headed toward her office, half-floating, her mind elsewhere. When she reached her desk, she found yet another message from Kostos— wishing her good luck during her yoga class that morning.

> KOSTOS: I'm about as unflexible as they come. You'd better teach me how to loosen up soon.

Nancy's cheeks burned, and she pressed her phone against her chest, trying to calm her heartbeat. Suddenly, there was a sharp knock at the door, and she turned to find Elsa in the crack, as Nancy had apparently been too lost in thought to close the door the entire way.

"You look over the moon about something," Elsa said, her smile mischievous.

Nancy placed her phone back on the table. "It's nothing. Just a good morning, is all."

Elsa narrowed her eyes. They'd known one another for too long for Nancy to get away with lying.

"Did you ever meet up with that Greek man we met at the Aquinnah Cliffside?"

Nancy scrunched up her face, giving herself away, as Elsa shrieked.

"Why have you kept that to yourself?"

Nancy leaned against her desk and raised her shoulders. "He's just a friend, really." Of course, friends didn't hold hands the way Kostos and Nancy had, energy burning in the air between them.

"I don't think that man ever wanted you to be his friend," Elsa said. "Are you seeing him again?"

Nancy tucked a curl behind her ear, not sure she wanted to say that she'd already seen him again yesterday and that he'd invited her to his vacation home that evening. It was her business, her mess.

But Nancy's thoughtful silence had given her away. "When!" Elsa demanded.

Nancy sighed. "I'm seeing him tonight. Apparently, he's a fantastic cook, and he wants to make a Greek dish for me."

Elsa shrieked into her hands. "Have you told Janine?"

"No! No, no. I don't want to distract Janine from her Venice adventures," Nancy said. "Have you heard about the scavenger hunt?"

"Only via text," Elsa admitted. "Maggie mentioned that Alyssa has completely fallen into the story, hardly coming up for air."

"That sounds like my Alyssa," Nancy said. "I'm sure Maggie is a bit at a distance, watching it all play out."

"All four of you are living out a movie," Elsa pointed

out. "You with your Greek romance, and the three of them with their Venice adventure."

After work that afternoon, Nancy returned to the Remington House, showered, and changed into a sundress. To calm her nerves, she drank half a glass of wine on the back porch, watching seagulls play, whizzing up and over the waves before landing staunchly on the sands again.

Nancy met Kostos downtown, where they planned to go for a walk, go grocery shopping, and eventually drive back to Kostos' beach house for dinner. Just like the previous two dates or whatever they were, Kostos arrived before Nancy, opening his arms to her as she approached. Nancy realized it had been a long time since she'd felt so at-home with a man, and she reveled in it, kissing his cheeks and hugging him deeply.

As they walked, Kostos told her a story about the repairman who'd come to the beach house that morning. "He came to fix the back porch door, but he ended up breaking two other things while there! I couldn't believe it. I've never seen a clumsier repairman."

Nancy laughed. "Did you fire him?"

"No! I'm a sucker. I decided to hire him to repair the stuff he broke."

"He's making more work for himself," Nancy pointed out.

"I honestly don't think it's that sinister," Kostos said. "If it is, I'm the biggest fool in the world."

Nancy paused on the boardwalk, smiling at him generously, her heart stirring. A part of her was terrified that she would just blurt out how much she liked him, just like that, without considering the consequences first.

But before she could, she heard her name.

"Nancy! Hey!" Henry, Janine's fiancé, appeared on the boardwalk, walking alongside a documentarian friend and previous colleague, Quentin Copperfield, who'd once been a popular nightly-news anchor before his recent move to Nantucket.

In fact, seeing Quentin Copperfield out on the boardwalk was thrilling for Nancy, who'd relied on him for the news for decades. Although she'd known Henry and Quentin were friendly, and that Alyssa was good friends with Quentin's daughter, she'd never seen them together.

"Henry, hello!" Nancy smiled nervously, eyeing handsome Quentin Copperfield. "What are you doing out here?"

"Just walking and talking," Henry said. "Have you met my friend Quentin Copperfield?"

"I haven't. My name is Nancy. And this is my friend…"

"Kostos." Kostos stuck out his hand dominantly and shook first Quentin's, then Henry's. Henry peered at Kostos curiously, probably ready to take this gossip to Janine immediately. Ugh.

"Rhonda at the fish restaurant mentioned she saw you with a handsome stranger recently," Henry said slyly to Nancy, teasing her. "I suppose you must be that man?"

"Who knows how many handsome strangers Nancy associates with?" Kostos quipped.

Laughing, Henry's face brightened.

"Your daughter is Janine, correct?" Quentin asked.

"She is," Nancy said. "My brilliant daughter."

"Henry was just telling me about this scavenger hunt in Venice. It sounds like a crazy adventure."

"It really does," Nancy said, glancing toward Kostos. "The story has gotten even weirder."

Kostos' eyes sparkled. "What happened?"

"They followed clues to a mausoleum, which led them to a cousin of theirs, who gave them a very old book, basically as big as a tome, wherein they were supposed to find 'clues.'" Nancy used air quotes and laughed at herself.

"Was the book written in Italian?" Kostos asked.

"Yes," Nancy said. "I don't know how they're managing this. I would have lost my head during the very first clue."

"And there's no end in sight to the game?" Kostos asked.

"Not that they can see," Nancy said. "Although, to be honest, I'm starting to miss my girls. I hope they figure this out soon and come on home. Henry, I'm sure you feel the same about Janine!"

Henry blushed and glanced at Quentin, who waved his hand.

"I wouldn't survive a day without my Catherine," Quentin said. "Even after twenty-plus years of marriage."

"It's only been about a week," Henry said with a sigh. "But yeah. I'm starting to get anxious. I hope they come back soon."

For a little while, Henry and Quentin updated Kostos and Nancy about their recent documentary projects and about the potential for them to work on a feature-length documentary soon. Kostos was curious, asking wonderful questions that kept the men engaged far longer than Nancy had wanted. Like a much younger woman, she found herself jealous, waiting for Henry and Quentin to leave so she could have Kostos to herself again. Wasn't that pathetic?

But later, in Kostos' vacation home kitchen, as she

sliced an onion with a very sharp knife, Kostos admitted he'd felt the same.

"They're fascinating men, absolutely," he said, scrubbing his hands with soap and water before he prepared the fish. "But I've met plenty of fascinating men. I've never met anyone like you."

Nancy's heart hammered in her chest. Suddenly frightened she would make a mistake and cut herself, she put the knife down and turned toward Kostos, unsure how to translate to him that she hadn't felt anything so invigorating in a very long time— that, prior to this arrival in her world, she'd been living vicariously through Alyssa, Maggie, and Janine. She didn't want to do that anymore.

"I haven't met anyone like you, either," Nancy breathed. "I hope that isn't too silly to say."

"Everything is silly at this stage of the game," Kostos said, his smile crooked. "But I am open to being a fool."

"So am I."

Kostos took a small step toward her. "It's funny how long life is, isn't it? It's filled with so many eras, so many opportunities for change."

"I never could have imagined it as a young woman." Nancy's voice wavered.

Kostos was close enough to take her hands in his. On the counter behind him, the fresh fish gleamed, pink and gray and fresh, ready for the skillet that was preheated on the stovetop. Neal had never cooked alongside Nancy, and Nancy would have never dreamed of such an arrangement. How nice to have someone beside her, preparing the feast. How nice to have a partner.

But Nancy didn't stay the night. Perhaps it was due to fear, or the fact that she had an early-morning yoga class, or because she wanted to wake up even earlier than that to talk to Janine on the phone. After they dined on the back porch, watching as the sky fuzzed to darkness and the stars punctuated the black, Nancy gathered her things, hugged Kostos goodbye, and got into her car, ready to drive back to the Remington House. It was only when she returned home, washed her face, and tucked herself into bed alone that Kostos texted her.

> **KOSTOS: I wish you would have stayed.**

But Nancy knew herself. She remembered the old days when she'd jumped into relationships too quickly, when she'd fallen in love too fast. She was grateful for a touch of naivety, as it allowed her to be open-hearted to this hope of romance. But being too naive, she knew, wasn't just stupid— it was self-destructive.

Chapter Nine

After more than a week in Venice, Janine, Alyssa, and Maggie had fallen into a gorgeous rhythm of sleeping, eating, walking, riding on water taxis and gondolas, and, of course, talking at-length about Teresa's game— one that Alyssa was determined to win.

It had been two days since Francesca had revealed the clue: "Paradiso Terrestre," a painting at the Gallerie dell'Accademia. Itching for the next clue, Alyssa dragged Janine and Maggie out of bed early that morning, fed them pastries, and chatted endlessly about the painting itself, which she'd learned had been painted by Jacopo Bassano in 1573.

"It's less than one hundred years after the first Cacciapaglia was buried in the mausoleum," Maggie pointed out. "Maybe Jacopo Bassano was involved with the family somehow? Maybe he married one of the women in the Cacciapaglia family?"

Alyssa's eyes were illuminated. "I was thinking the same thing! But I have no idea how we can prove that. There's not very much information on the painting online, at least nothing in English. And I think Teresa wants us to think outside the box again, you know? Maybe the clue has nothing to do with the painting's history. Maybe it's something about what's featured in the painting itself. Or maybe there's something on the frame?"

Alyssa buzzed with excitement all the way to the museum, which was located on the south bank of the Grand Canal. According to the informational pamphlet Janine picked up in the entryway, the museum had been founded in 1750— twenty-six years before the birth of the United States. The ornate building the museum was housed in, however, was far older— built in approximately 1343.

"1343!" Maggie hissed, lifting her chin to take in the impressively high ceilings.

"The top floor has paintings from 1300 to 1600," Alyssa chimed in. "That'll be where it is."

Although Janine wanted to peruse the ground floor, to fall into these impossibly old works of art, she scampered after Alyssa as quickly as she could, with Maggie hot on her heels.

"I've never seen a pregnant woman move so quickly," Maggie huffed. "I thought she was only two years younger than me! I didn't know she was planning to train for the Olympics during her pregnancy."

Janine laughed, whipping up the staircase to the top floor, where already Alyssa slipped through tourists, scouting for the painting. And not long afterward, they approached it, walking slowly, with reverence.

The painting itself was exquisite, featuring two naked figures— a man and a woman, whom Janine assumed were Adam and Eve. They were featured in a gorgeous and lush garden with the sky overhead looking dangerous, wrought with pain and anger. Animals cowered in the corner— lambs, a bunny, and a chicken, and birds were perched in the trees.

Alyssa crossed and uncrossed her arms, studying the painting. Janine watched Alyssa for some sign she understood the painting or why Teresa had chosen this as a clue. Maggie looked at it for a second or two before collapsing on the bench in front of it, clearly exhausted. Around them, tourists milled through the hall, pausing in front of each painting.

"The frame is normal, I guess," Alyssa muttered, mostly to herself. "And the painting is extraordinary, of course. But I don't see anything about it that makes me think of Teresa..."

Janine placed her hand on Alyssa's shoulder. "You know, if we don't figure this out, it's okay," she said. "It's been so nice here in Venice with my girls."

Alyssa's eyes snapped toward Janine, surprised. "You want to give up?"

The way Alyssa asked it reminded Janine of when she'd been a little girl, asking her mother or father if she could stay up just a little bit longer, if only to be with them. It had always broken Janine's heart a little bit, as she'd always been fully aware of the fact that Alyssa would, one day, grow up. Now, she had.

But before Alyssa said anything else, a tour stepped through the hall, headed by a late-twenty-something Italian man who spoke perfect English. He was dressed smartly in a mustard button-down and slacks, and his thick hair was wild and ruffled, erupting from his ears in black curls.

"This painting in particular," he was telling his tour,

"was painted by Jacopo Bassano and completed in 1573. As you can see, it features Adam and Eve in the garden, much like many, many other paintings of that time. But this painting stands out for us today for one reason— back in 1867, this painting was stolen from the Gallerie dell'Accademia."

Members of the tour gasped with appreciation, removed their cell phones from their pockets, and took photographs furiously.

"Who stole it?" A man in the tour asked, his eyebrows high.

The Italian tour guide laced his fingers together, clearly pleased with his performance and its effect.

"His name was Mauricio Gionnocaro," the tour guide went on. "And he was rumored to be, at that time, in charge of a secret society based here in Venice. That secret society potentially served as puppeteers for a number of religious and political heads up until quite recently, when it was rumored that the secret society completely disbanded. As their members upheld their secrecy above all things, it was often difficult for historians to get to the bottom of what really happened. We still don't know much to this day.

"But thirty-five years after Mauricio stole the painting, his daughter returned it to the museum," the tour guide went on. "She was disillusioned with her father, and she said a number of choice things about his 'special operation' and his 'delusions.' I suppose, for me, at least, that makes it clear that this painting was instrumental to the secret society in some way. Viewers often report feeling a definite power within the paint strokes, the colors, and the images themselves."

Suddenly, a familiar voice interrupted the tour.

"I'm sorry. May I ask a question?" It was Alyssa, hovering along the edge of the tour, trying to get closer to the tour guide.

"Of course." The tour guide smiled.

"Did this man, Mauricio Gionnocaro, have anything to do with the Cacciapaglia family?" Alyssa asked.

The tour guide tilted his head with curiosity. "They are certainly both very old families within the region. I don't know off-hand if they had or have anything to do with one another, but I'm sure a better historian knows."

"Is there somewhere I could learn about that?" Alyssa asked. "And more about this secret society?"

The tour guide seemed unaccustomed to people actually caring that much about what he said. He stepped around the rest of the tour to get closer to Alyssa, and, if Janine wasn't mistaken, his face fell slightly when he noticed she was pregnant.

"The Gionnocaro Museum is not far down the Grand Canal," he explained. "It was their family home for centuries, until recently. There, you can learn as much as we know about the secret society— which, as I mentioned, isn't a lot. Perhaps someone who works there could tell you more about the Cacciapaglia and Gionnocaro connection."

Alyssa's smile was electric. It was clear that she knew she'd stumbled onto gold. "Thank you so much. What is your name?"

Janine's heart flipped over. For years, she'd watched Alyssa stumble through men, through relationships, without any sense of belonging. To see her eyes alight like this during a conversation with a handsome Italian man thrilled her— even as it terrified her. For she knew most men wouldn't date a pregnant woman. They wouldn't even consider it.

"My name is Nico," he said. "And you are?"

"Alyssa." Alyssa stuck out her hand and shook Nico's hand, there in front of everyone, as though she'd forgotten the rest of the world existed.

"Well, do be in touch if you learn anything, Alyssa," Nico said. "Are you a historian? A student?"

"Sort of both and sort of neither," Alyssa said with a shrug.

"Vague! Wonderful." Nico palmed the back of his neck and looked at the rest of his tour, whose eyes had begun to glaze. He then clapped his hands and said, "All right, everyone. Let's proceed to the next room. I think you're going to recognize this next painting. I'm assuming you've heard of Michaelangelo?"

As the tour headed into the next room, Alyssa hurried back to Janine and Maggie, where she threw her arms around both of them. Janine laughed.

"I can't believe this," Maggie said, shaking her head. "We have to go to yet another location?"

"It's all a part of the fun, Mags."

"Let's get lunch," Janine suggested. "And maybe read up a bit more on this secret society before we head to the next museum right away?"

"I'm in no rush," Alyssa assured them. "I don't want this to be over yet."

"You'd love to drag this out for years!" Maggie said.

"Maybe not years," Alyssa said. "But it's a wonderful distraction. I haven't remembered how much my feet and back hurt in hours."

"Speak for yourself." Maggie smiled, clearly confused

with her sister's joy yet slightly invigorated by it. "All right. Lunch. What's on the docket?"

"Pizza or pasta!" Alyssa cried.

"Ugh. It never changes," Maggie said, heading toward the staircase before turning back to wink at Janine and Alyssa. Who in their right mind could resist pizza or pasta? Janine hadn't raised her daughters to think that way. They knew to appreciate the finer things in life. They knew to eat divine dishes, engage with gorgeous music, to say yes to dessert. Even Maggie, the more health-conscious of the two, had gotten ridiculously good at baking on her quest to create the finer things in life herself.

Downstairs in the foyer, right before they entered the splintering heat of the August afternoon, Janine laced her fingers through her girls' and said, "I love you, you know."

And together, in unison, her girls looked at her and said, "We love you, too." And there, beneath the Italian sun, Janine felt weightless and alive, apt to float along the canals of that gorgeous city for the rest of her days.

Chapter Ten

Elsa knocked on Nancy's office door at ten-thirty in the morning and, upon entering, beamed through the shadows, clearly eager for Nancy's gossip regarding Kostos. But since their third, fourth, and fifth dates, Nancy had kept quiet— not wanting to taint such a gorgeous time. For reasons she still wasn't sure of, she and Kostos had still not kissed nor slept over at one another's houses. But that, she felt, was okay. She was just grateful for the attention, for the floaty feeling that kept her adrenalized throughout the day.

"Good morning! Tonight, Bruce and I are going to have a spontaneous barbecue at our place," Elsa said. "Do you want to join?"

Nancy's chest opened up at the thought. It had been ages since she'd seen some of the members of the family, probably since their goodbye brunch for Lucy, and she was ready to sit, drink wine, watch the sun slip into an orange sea, and celebrate another beautiful summer's day.

"I would love it," Nancy said. And then, for reasons

she would never be sure of, she heard herself ask, "Do you mind if I bring a friend?"

"We would love it! Please, bring him by. I ran into Henry the other day, and he said Kostos is clearly smitten with you." Elsa did a little dance in the doorway.

"Goodness, the gossip on this island is out of control," Nancy said, her stomach filled with butterflies.

"We all love you," Elsa reminded her. "And yes. We're all just a little obsessed with each other, aren't we?" She smiled. "Oh! I meant to tell you. We hired Stan Ellis to do some repairs downstairs, if you want to say hello."

"Very much so!" Nancy stood up immediately, surprised to hear Stan's name again. Nearly two years ago, Stan had saved Nancy and Carmella during a hurricane, whisking them to safety as the floods and winds had come. That particular storm had destroyed Stan's home, and Nancy had offered him a room at the Katama Lodge and Wellness Spa until he'd been able to restore his place along the water. During that time, Stan and Nancy had become fast friends, frequently playing cards and listening to music. They'd even watched a film together once, seated only a few feet apart on Nancy's office couch as her computer had streamed *Love, Actually*. Stan had cried.

Stan's life had never been easy. Since Nancy's arrival on the island, she'd known of the disaster of Stan's life, which had happened back in 1996. At the time, Stan had been having an affair with a married woman named Anna Sheridan, the mother of Susan, Christine, and Lola Sheridan. Late one night, Stan had wrecked their boat, and Anna had drowned— abandoning her children and her husband and leaving Stan in the wrong.

As a result, Stan had been something of a pariah on

the island for decades. But Nancy knew what it was like to have made many, many mistakes. She didn't hold it against him, especially now that she knew the goodness of his heart.

Nancy padded downstairs to find Stan atop a ladder, investigating the hanging light fixture in the hallway nearest the library. Not wanting to startle him, Nancy waited for a little while, watching as he fiddled, before she finally cleared her throat and forced his eyes toward her.

"Nancy!" Stan's smile was immediate, and he abandoned his work and hurried down the ladder to hug her. "It's been a little while, hasn't it?"

"It sure has," Nancy said. "Where have you been?"

"It's just been so nice, having my home back," Stan admitted. "Tommy's been over frequently, fishing with me this summer. I suppose I've let the days get away from me."

"I can understand that."

"Of course! You've got that big house filled with people."

Nancy winced. "Right now, I'm an empty nester, I'm afraid."

"You're kidding! Everyone left?"

"My daughter and granddaughters are in Italy right now, and everyone else has moved out," Nancy explained. "I feel like a ghost in that big, old place."

"Goodness." Stan hesitated, and his eyes glistened in a way that made Nancy question, not for the first time, if Stan had feelings for her.

But that was impossible. They'd been friends for two years at this point. They'd been there for one another through frantic, truly terrible times. That negated any romance.

Besides, she was already falling for someone else.

"Thanks for coming in to do some work," Nancy added, taking a small step away from him.

"This place was my home for a little while," Stan said. "I'm happy to keep it up any way I can."

"I hope it was okay for you, living here."

"It was certainly a different experience," Stan said with a laugh. "I never thought I'd live anywhere but my shack, alone. And then, suddenly, I was living alongside all these women at the Lodge! Keeping to myself, of course. Even still, so many of them welcomed me and asked me about myself. I had many emotional conversations about my life and, well, about what happened in my past, here at the Lodge. But these women, they weren't judgmental. I learned so much from them."

Nancy reached out to take Stan's wrist, which she squeezed gently, overwhelmed with what he'd said. It was rare for Stan to discuss what had happened in 1996, even in round-about terms. Speaking this way was perhaps proof that, slowly but surely, he'd begun to heal.

Kostos agreed to come to Elsa's barbecue whole-heartedly. "I've spent so much of my time here on the island alone! A party is beyond my wildest dreams."

A true gentleman, Kostos picked Nancy up from the Remington House and drove her down the road to Elsa's new place, which she and Bruce had had built as a sign of the strength of their new-ish relationship and the next era of their lives together. Nancy had made potato salad and brought a bottle of chilled rosé, which she cracked open immediately on the back porch, perhaps due to nerves about her family meeting Kostos.

But she shouldn't have worried. Kostos was incredibly social, shaking everyone's hands, asking them about themselves, and congratulating Elsa and Bruce on their gorgeous new home. Unsurprisingly, Susan Sheridan was already seated at the porch table— the daughter of the woman Stan had been having an affair with— and she raised a glass to Nancy, smiling. Susan was Bruce's partner at the law firm, a truly unique and powerful woman on the island. Although officially the Sheridan's had forgiven Stan, Nancy knew it wasn't so simple.

"How are you, Nancy?" Susan asked.

"I'm fantastic," Nancy said just as Kostos came up beside her, wrapped his arm around her shoulders, and leaned forward to shake Susan's hand.

"I'm Kostos!"

"Susan. Where are you from? Greece?"

"Guilty as charged," Kostos said.

"And what has brought you to Martha's Vineyard?"

"Dreams of a better life in America!" Kostos said, faking bravado. "But I have a hunch something else will keep me here." He turned slightly to lock eyes with Nancy, who blushed.

"It's a magical place filled with magical people," Susan assured him. "I lived away for twenty-five years before I came back."

"That's a very long time to be away from home," Kostos said somberly.

"Too long," Susan agreed.

Carmella came up the back porch steps, her hand over her pregnant stomach, although she was hardly showing. "Nancy! Can you believe the latest development with the Venice scavenger hunt?"

Kostos perked up. "You haven't told me!"

Nancy laughed. "Apparently, the next clue involves a secret society in Venice. At least, that's what Alyssa thinks. I was on the phone with her this morning, and she gabbed and gabbed about what she'd learned so far about this secret society."

"What has she learned?" Susan asked. "It's not every day I learn about a secret Italian society!"

"Apparently, they were founded back in 789 A.C.," Nancy explained, still flabbergasted at the year. "They sought control in their communities, their religious sects, and within their relationships, and they probably turned to religious texts for guidance. Apparently, there are rumors of secret rituals that they conducted in order to speak to God himself, although Alyssa couldn't find specifics."

"It sounds like a movie," Susan said.

"Right? I was thinking that," Kostos said. "But I'm from Greece! Thousands of years ago, we had hundreds of gods! So, I guess I shouldn't be too surprised about what my neighbor country was up to."

Everyone at the table chuckled. Elsa floated out onto the back porch with a pitcher of lemonade, asking if anyone needed anything as Kostos cuddled Nancy closer. Her nostrils filled with his smell, and her heart felt weightless and soft.

"Well, it sounds like it's all been a wonderful distraction," Carmella suggested, clearly speaking of Lucy.

"I think it has been," Nancy offered. "Alyssa begged me to come out to Venice to continue the hunt with them."

"Oh! You should go!" Elsa's eyes widened. "How often in life do you get an opportunity like this?"

Kostos' face was stony in a way Nancy couldn't fully read. *Was he jealous?*

"When would you leave?" he asked, his voice wavering.

Nancy felt flustered. "I haven't booked anything yet."

Kostos tilted his head. "The thing is, I have a flight to go back to Greece in about a week."

Nancy was suddenly stricken. As the rest of the table turned to one another for private conversations, she lowered her voice to whisper, "You didn't mention that!"

"I won't be gone forever," Kostos said. "I have a few family matters to attend to."

Nancy nodded. "It always comes down to family, doesn't it?"

"I knew you'd understand that," Kostos said, bowing his head. "Listen. A thought just came to me out of the blue. And you can say no if you want to."

Nancy frowned, her heart thudding.

"What if we flew to Venice together? That way, I can see that gorgeous city again and meet the rest of your family before I head on to Greece?"

Nancy's lips parted with surprise. She had not expected this. Then again, she hadn't expected anything surrounding Kostos. He was a complete outlier.

"I know we just met each other," Kostos hurried to add, "and I know there's so much we haven't discussed. But to be honest with you, Nancy, you'd be doing me a favor. I absolutely detest that transatlantic flight. When I do it by myself, I spend most of it terrified and glued to my chair."

It was difficult for Nancy to imagine Kostos in such a

state. Her heart melted at the fear that now echoed from his eyes.

"It isn't too difficult to get over to Greece from Venice," Kostos finished. "What do you say?"

Nancy didn't hesitate. "I think it sounds wonderful to have company. Let's do it."

After all, what did she have to lose? Even if Kostos had only been a friend rather than someone she was falling for, she would have said yes in a heartbeat. Kostos had just revealed a weakness, a devastating interior flaw that often made his overnight flights unbearable. She would do anything to take that pain away. She had to.

Chapter Eleven

Janine tip-toed to the kitchen a couple of mornings after their museum visit to get a glass of water, only to discover all the lights on, Alyssa's head on the kitchen table, and library books flung open in front of her, only some of them in English. Her laptop was propped open, as well, on a translation website, where it seemed like Alyssa had been painstakingly typing passages from Italian books to get a better sense of this crazy Italian secret society. Ugh.

Janine shook Alyssa awake gently. "Alyssa? Honey?"

Alyssa's eyes fluttered open, and then she burst awake. "Mom! What time is it?"

"It's four-thirty," Janine said, stifling a yawn.

"Oh. Ugh." Alyssa rubbed her eyes as Janine bent to peer at the strange paintings in the Italian books, many of which showed the "secret rituals" the society used to orchestrate.

"You didn't go to bed at all?" Janine asked.

"I got obsessed with learning about this stuff," Alyssa said. "I just kept going."

"You have to take care of yourself, sweetie." Janine wrapped a curl around Alyssa's ear.

"I know. Don't tell Maggie about this, okay?" Alyssa closed her computer slowly.

"Why don't you sleep in a little bit?" Janine urged. "There's no rush on going to Mauricio's house. You can sleep in and have a late breakfast. I think it's supposed to rain all day…" Janine paused to listen for the patter of rain on the windows. Although it was inky black, she could feel the canals filling, the city slumbering beneath and above all that water. "Maybe it's a good day to rest."

Reluctantly, Alyssa agreed, yet demanded that the books remain open where she'd left them and that nobody touch them. Janine translated this information to Maggie a few hours later, when they'd both awoken for morning tea, watching the rain from the kitchen counter.

"Your sister doesn't want us to touch those books."

"Where are we supposed to eat breakfast?" Maggie asked with a laugh.

Eventually, Janine and Maggie donned raincoats and headed out into the gray morning. There beneath an awning, they ate chocolate croissants as Janine drank a small espresso and Maggie had tea, watching as tourists tried to make the best of one of their fleeting mornings in Venice, despite the downpour.

It was rare for Janine to be alone with one of her daughters, as they were often glued at the hip, the very best of friends despite their differences. It had been that way for years.

"I just got some information," Maggie began, her voice soft and lyrical. "I don't know what to make of it."

"Tell me." Janine placed her espresso cup back in its saucer with a clack.

Maggie's face was pinched. "Rex is engaged."

Janine's jaw dropped. Quickly, her hand found Maggie's on her lap, and she held it tenderly as though it was a tiny, breakable egg. "I can't believe this."

Maggie blinked back tears, trying and failing to tug her lips into a smile. "I shouldn't be the one who's angry. I'm pregnant with another man's child, for crying out loud. And that happened not long after we broke up."

"He was cheating on you, Maggie."

Maggie winced, and for a moment, Janine wondered if that had been the wrong thing to bring up. It was never easy to consider the depths of someone's betrayal like that. She knew that better than most.

"I loved him for a long time," Maggie offered, swiping beneath her eye to catch a tear.

"And a part of you always will," Janine said. "I mean, look at me! In Venice, visiting your father's family!"

Maggie's shoulders dropped. "You're doing it for us. For Alyssa and me. I know that."

"But I'm also doing it for me," Janine told her. "I lived with and loved your father for decades. Coming here feels like finding the final piece in a thousand-piece puzzle. It feels like making peace."

On the canal in front of them, yet another gondola purred past, and the rower sang gently an Italian song everyone seemed to know well: "Azzurro."

"It's bizarre that the baby Alyssa is carrying is the one Rex and I made together," Maggie added, sounding wistful. "And even more bizarre that Rex would rather pretend it never happened."

"Babies come into the world for all sorts of reasons," Janine said. "I think it's a blessing that Rex wants to stay out of this baby's business. Imagine having to deal with him all the time!" Janine shook her head. "I knew so many families in New York who divorced. They had to coordinate pick-ups and drop-offs, had to restructure holidays and vacation times. Because Rex is stepping away, you and David can plan your family however you want."

"And Alyssa," Maggie added, her eyes sparkling. "I'll never forget the sacrifice she made for me. And I hope beyond anything she knows she's a part of our family, too."

"I think she does."

Alyssa didn't wake up till two in the afternoon, when she emerged from the shadows of the upstairs hallway and walked slowly, like a ghost, down the staircase. Maggie and Janine were in the living room, both reading in comfortable house clothes, enjoying the silence in one another's company.

"There she is," Maggie said, closing her book. "Our very own Indiana Jones!"

"Ha ha." Alyssa rolled her eyes sarcastically. "You didn't touch the Italian books on the table, did you?"

"We did not," Maggie assured her.

"Did you find any connection to the Cacciapaglias?" Janine asked.

Alyssa slumped into the chair beside Maggie and rubbed her temples. "Nothing so far."

"I think we should take the day off from the scavenger hunt," Maggie announced.

Alyssa gave her a nervous side-eye. "And do what?"

Maggie shrugged. "Eat? Go to piazzas? Go to another museum? Eat some more?"

Janine sensed that Maggie was trying to distract both of them: Maggie from Rex's new engagement and Alyssa from her newfound obsessions. They both looked at her as though for permission.

"You know me. I'm always happy to eat my way through this city," Janine said with a laugh.

And eat they did. As it was only two, Alyssa hurried to dress, and they wandered to the nearby piazza for a gorgeous late lunch: fresh fish, salad, homemade bread, and sparkling juice. Bit by bit, both Alyssa and Maggie seemed rejuvenated, telling jokes and old stories.

"Now that we're here in Italy, I've been thinking of even more baby names to add to the mix," Alyssa said mischievously.

"Uh oh." Maggie put her fork down, clearly regretting she'd told Alyssa she could have a say.

"What about Leonardo?"

"Ugh," Maggie groaned.

"Okay, okay. Cleopatra?"

Janine laughed into her napkin. "Queen of the Nile?"

"We could call her Cleo," Alyssa said. "Or, if one of them is a baby boy, we can call him Plato?"

"Plato's from Greece!" Maggie shot back. "Neither of those last two work with your Italian theme."

"It's all Greek to me," Alyssa said, waving her hands.

"Funny joke." Maggie rolled her eyes.

"That reminds me," Janine interjected. "I just got a weird text from your grandmother. Apparently, she wants to visit next week— and bring a friend along."

Alyssa and Maggie leaned over the table, captivated.

"What kind of friend?" Maggie demanded.

"What do you mean, what kind of friend? Grandma

knows how to work it. Don't you remember her at your wedding? She flirted with everyone!"

"But she really hasn't been with anyone since Neal died," Maggie offered tentatively. "And if this is a romantic interest, it's a big deal. Really big." She nodded toward Janine, who felt similarly.

"I texted Carmella about it," Janine said. "Apparently, they all met him at a family party, and he seems great. And—" Janine drummed her hands on the table for dramatic effect. "He's Greek."

"What!" Alyssa and Maggie said in unison.

"How did Grandma meet a Greek guy in Martha's Vineyard?" Alyssa demanded.

"Apparently, she met him while out for a glass of wine with Carmella and Elsa at the Aquinnah Cliffside Overlook," Janine said. "Carmella says he's handsome and seems to really like her a lot. He's visiting family in Greece, and they decided to say what the heck and fly across the Atlantic together. He hasn't been in Venice in a while, and he wants to explore with us, spend the night, then head to Greece."

"Incredible," Maggie said. "It sounds too good to be true."

Suddenly, from across the piazza came the sound of Alyssa's name. Alyssa burst around, her hair flying, and stared toward the source of the sound. Janine followed her gaze to find a familiar and very handsome man striding toward them— the tour guide from the museum.

"I can't believe he remembered your name," Maggie whispered, taking the words right out of Janine's mouth.

But already, Alyssa was up, adjusting her shoulders behind her. Unfortunately, this only served to press her pregnant belly out even more.

"Nico! Hi!" Alyssa smiled.

"I thought that was you! Good thing, too, since I just yelled your name in front of about fifty people." Nico cackled at himself, his cheeks reddening from embarrassment.

"I'm sure you're used to embarrassing yourself," Alyssa said. "You're a tour guide at a museum, remember?"

"Actually, that's the place in the world where I embarrass myself the least. Everyone defers to my knowledge and doesn't question me. Out in the real world, on the other hand? I'm a lost cause."

Alyssa giggled as, over the table, Janine and Maggie locked eyes and shared a secretive smile.

"Have you made it to the Mauricio Giannocaro house yet?" Nico asked.

Alyssa shook her head. "No, but I went to the library yesterday and checked out about a million books about the family and the secret society, hoping to get a better sense of the connection to the Cacciapaglias."

"Oh. Nice." Nico paused. "But you don't speak Italian, do you?"

"I'm using a translation service," Alyssa said. "It's taking quite a while, obviously."

"Obviously," Nico said with a laugh. "What's the interest with the Cacciapaglias?" Janine noticed that at no time did he look down at Alyssa's pregnant stomach.

Alyssa blushed. "Technically, we're Cacciapaglias." She gestured toward Maggie, still seated beside her. "Our grandmother was Teresa."

Nico's jaw dropped. For a moment, Janine was petrified he would say that he was related to Teresa, that she was his cousin or aunt or something like that.

"I'm so sorry for your loss," Nico said. "Teresa was a remarkable and very quirky woman. She used to come into the museum all the time." He paused, frowning, then added, "She used to stare at that painting all the time. 'Paradiso Terrestre.'"

"Did she ever say anything about it?" Alyssa asked.

"No. We spoke often, but never about the painting. She always had a story to tell and always had time to sit for a coffee and chat. I adored her. I never had a grandmother of my own, as they both died when I was very young, and Teresa has that place in my heart." Nico patted his chest gently.

Alyssa's eyes were bright, tender. It was clearer than ever that she was into him.

"Anyway, how much longer are you in Venice?" Nico asked.

"A bit longer," Alyssa said. "We're living at Teresa's old place. She gave us a sort of scavenger hunt. If we win, we get whatever she left us in her will."

Nico's eyes sparkled. "That sounds like something she would do. What happens if you lose?"

"We won't," Alyssa answered simply.

Nico laughed. "Um. Maybe this is weird, but can I have your number? I'm on my way somewhere, but I'd love to meet up before you go and maybe talk more about Teresa."

"We're eager to hear about her!" Alyssa typed her number into Nico's phone, her cheeks now completely crimson.

Nico said goodbye and fled the scene as though he wanted to get away from them as quickly as possible. Just as Alyssa collapsed back in her chair, clearly lost in thought, her phone buzzed with a text from Nico.

"That was fast," Maggie said, sipping her sparkling juice.

"It's crazy he knew Teresa," Alyssa offered.

"Everyone seems to know everyone else in this city," Janine said. "It feels like a village."

Alyssa remained quiet for a moment, her eyes lost, peering somewhere behind Janine's head, probably at nothing at all.

"Admit it, Alyssa," Maggie interjected. "You like him."

Alyssa waved her hand. "I can't like him. Come on."

"What are you talking about?" Janine asked.

"I mean, look at me." Alyssa gestured toward her stomach, six months pregnant. "It's only going to get bigger."

"He doesn't seem to care," Maggie said. "And maybe you can explain to him the situation. That you're doing it for me."

Alyssa raised her shoulders. "It's dangerous. What if I start to like him, like him? My life is in Martha's Vineyard. I'm going to be there for baby Galileo's childhood and messy teenage years. I'm going to be there for their wedding! I can't get involved with someone who lives in Italy. It's too chaotic from the get-go."

"Alyssa, why don't you just go on a date with him?" Maggie said with a sigh. "A date never hurt anyone."

Alyssa was quiet and contemplative for a moment. "But it did, Maggie."

Janine frowned, suddenly recognizing the true problem here. The last man Alyssa had let herself get really involved with had attacked her on that private plane in November 2021— which was fewer than two years ago and still relatively fresh. It clicked for Maggie, too.

"You know, not everyone is like that guy," Maggie offered. "Some of them are really worth your time."

"Not ones like Rex," Alyssa said.

Maggie sighed, her eyes misting. "Okay. There are a lot of bad ones, too. But the love I've found with David has been totally worth it. And I know there's love to be found out there for you, too."

Alyssa's lower lip quivered. Janine hurried to take her hand over the table. "Honey, why haven't you mentioned this lately?"

"I tried to bury it as deep as I could," Alyssa said.

"Right. Like that always works." Maggie gave her sister a look.

"Would you be interested in trying online therapy?" Janine asked, tilting her head. "You could start right away with someone I know in New York. She's brilliant, honey. And she could accommodate our schedule here in Venice."

Alyssa looked hesitant.

"We all need a little bit of help, Alyssa," Maggie said. "We've been through a lot the past few years. And now, right before the babies come? We need to prepare ourselves mentally. We need to get really, really strong." Maggie paused, stuttering to add, "Maybe Nico isn't the guy you end up with for the rest of time. But he seems kind and slightly nerdy, and I think he probably knows where all the best restaurants in Venice are. Why don't you give him a chance? Maybe you'll regret it if you don't."

Chapter Twelve

But that night, after a great deal of poking and prodding, Alyssa did, in fact, text Nico. Immediately afterward, she flung the phone to the table, laced her fingers together, and shrieked as Maggie and Janine cackled. Janine felt caught up in their twenty-something universe, lost in the chaos of not-knowing so much of their lives yet. She felt one of them, to a point.

"It's going to be okay!" Maggie cupped Alyssa's elbow.

"What if it's not a date? What if I got the wrong idea?" Alyssa demanded.

"I don't think there's any mistaking what kind of look he gave you," Janine said.

"Aren't all Italians like that? Ridiculously romantic? Like something out of a movie?" Alyssa asked.

"Why don't you go and find out?" Maggie said.

Alyssa's phone buzzed on the table, making all of her Italian books vibrate, and she shrieked again, picked up the phone, and read: **"Alyssa! So glad to hear from**

Summer Rush

you. I have tomorrow off. Would you like to take a stroll and maybe have dinner?"

"That is a date, honey," Maggie said as Alyssa pressed her phone against her chest.

Janine recognized the look Alyssa gave them. It echoed her own two years ago, when she'd thought she would never have a chance at romance again. But at twenty-four, Alyssa had a whole lot of living left to do. Didn't she see that?

That night, Alyssa didn't stay up, obsessing over the Italian books and the Gionnocaro family. Instead, she fell asleep early, calling it "beauty sleep," and woke Janine up with a bang at eight o'clock sharp.

"Mom? It's an emergency. I don't have anything to wear."

Janine rubbed the sleep from her eyes as Alyssa collapsed on the other side of her bed. In her big sleep t-shirt and her biker shorts, she looked sloppy and casual, just as she always did at the Remington House.

"None of my pretty dresses fit," Alyssa admitted, speaking to the ceiling.

Janine reached across the bed and wrapped her hand around Alyssa's slender wrist. "Then I guess we'd better go shopping. What do you think?"

The boutiques in Venice opened their doors at eleven that morning. The three Potter women stood outside the first, which came highly recommended by an old friend of Janine's from the Upper West Side, then streamed through the doors upon entry, headed straight for the maxi dresses.

"I need something elegant. Something that sort-of, kind-of conceals the baby bump— or else makes me look really powerful with the baby bump?" Alyssa pinched several fabrics, frowning. "Maybe a mustard yellow? A navy blue?

It only took four stores, eighteen trips in and out of dressing rooms, and two meltdowns before Janine, Maggie, and Alyssa decided that this was the one: a forest green cut low over Alyssa's chest yet flowing angelically over her calves. With a strappy sandal, she looked like a goddess.

But Alyssa wasn't the only one who bought something. Maggie made sure to purchase a few baby-bump-friendly outfits, and Janine opted for a navy-blue dress with long sleeves, which she imagined herself wearing into autumn, remembering the beauty of these Italian days.

Back at the villa, Janine made them sandwiches with homemade bread, Italian sausage, and fresh, light cheese, and they ate and chatted as Alyssa buzzed with adrenaline, asking questions like, "What do people talk about on dates?"

Due to nerves, Alyssa called her cousin, Cole, a few minutes before Nico's arrival. In the next room, Janine eavesdropped, her heart swelling at the love Alyssa and Cole had for one another. Alyssa had been instrumental in helping Cole through the numerous difficulties he'd had since his father's death. Now that Cole had fallen in love with Aria, Janine hoped his stability would bleed over into Alyssa's life.

"Cole? What do you and Aria talk about?" Alyssa laughed at herself. "I know. I sound insane. I also know that you and Aria met on a sailboat in the middle of the ocean, which means you had a lot more to talk about than most couples."

Janine would have loved to hear Cole's advice on the

other end of the line. Whatever it was, it seemed to calm Alyssa considerably, and by the time Nico knocked on the door at four that afternoon, Alyssa seemed stable and at ease. In the doorway, they hugged one another, and a warm joy flooded Janine's body.

Not long after Alyssa left on her date with Nico, there was a knock on the door. It was Francesca, Teresa's secretary.

"Good afternoon! It's probably strange that I keep dropping by like this. I came to this house nearly every day for twelve years. It's bizarre that I'm no longer needed," she said.

"Would you like to come in?" Janine stepped back, opening the door wider.

Francesca waved her hand. "No. But it's good you're here. I want to invite you to a small family party tonight. Your cousin, Eva, will be there, as will several other Cacciapaglias, all of whom are very curious about you."

Janine knew better than to refuse an offer of food from an Italian. It wasn't just rude, it was idiotic, as they were some of the most brilliant home chefs in the world. "We won't miss it. What's the address?"

That evening at seven-thirty, Janine and Maggie entered a water taxi and floated down-canal toward Francesca's family home, which was located on the mainland, several streets away from where "proper" Venice began. This stood to reason, Janine supposed. Francesca worked as a secretary, which meant her family just didn't have the wealth of someone like Teresa. Still, other Cacciapaglias would be at the party, which meant that Francesca's family was still incredibly respected in the community— a part of the fabric of the very, very old and historic place. Perhaps the money rules in New York City didn't apply here. In New York, if you had money, you didn't deign to speak to people who didn't.

Well, Jack had, she remembered. He'd come up to a poor, young waitress. And he'd changed her life forever. How complicated.

Just like the rest of Venice, Francesca's family home was very old, made of a clay-like material Janine had never seen in the United States. Before they had the chance to knock on the door, Francesca opened it and called out in Italian to the others in the house to announce their arrival. She then kissed first Janine on the cheeks, then Maggie. As they followed after her, Maggie whispered in Janine's ear, "I don't know if I'll ever get used to the cheek-kissing thing. I guess I'm not really Italian!"

As they breezed through the house, Francesca introduced them to a stream of her own family members, along with four Cacciapaglias— Teresa's second niece, a second-cousin, a second-cousin once removed, as well as Teresa's first cousin, who was in his nineties and hardly spoke to anyone as he sat in the corner, his eyes glinting mischievously, almost like a little boy's.

"Tell us," Francesca's sister said, clasping her hands together, "has Teresa sent you to all corners of the city?"

Janine laughed. "She's certainly run us around."

"And in your condition!" Francesca's sister eyed Maggie nervously.

"Don't worry," Maggie assured her. "I'm not even as pregnant as my sister, and she hasn't slowed down once."

Francesca ushered them into the dining room, where they sat alongside family members, most of whom squabbled in Italian before taking small breaks to speak to them in bright English. As Francesca came in with a heaping pot of pasta, she paused and said, "Where is that sister of yours?" to which Maggie explained, "She's on a date!"

Francesca's sister cried out. "Who! Tell us! We know everyone in this city."

Maggie and Janine exchanged glances.

"He works at the Gallerie dell'Accademia," Janine explained. "I believe his name was..."

"Federico? Gio? Nico?" Francesca spouted.

"Nico," Maggie affirmed.

Francesca breathed a sigh of relief. "Oh. Good! He's wonderful."

"He adored Teresa," another family member said. "Funny that you met him."

"Alyssa interrupted his tour to ask him questions about a painting for Teresa's scavenger hunt," Maggie said.

Francesca's eyes glistened. "That must be another part of Teresa's plan!"

Janine stifled a laugh, knowing that those who knew Teresa well respected her "seeing eye" in a way she, a doubting American, never could.

To add drama to the night, Alyssa appeared around nine-thirty— a time when Janine, Maggie, and the rest of the family were stuffed to the gills, overwhelmed with wine, and praying Francesca wouldn't serve them too much chocolatey dessert. Maggie had texted Alyssa the address, telling her to swing by when she was finished.

"Look who it is!" Francesca led a red-cheeked Alyssa into the dining room.

Immediately, everyone in the dining room peppered her with questions about her date, about Nico, about whether or not he'd acted like a gentleman. Alyssa tossed her head, howling, "They can't keep a secret to save their lives!"

Another chair was procured, and Francesca forced it in between Maggie and Janine, both of whom hugged Alyssa. In Janine's arms, her youngest seemed small, frightened, and Janine caught her eye, curious, suddenly fearful that Nico had done something wrong. Sensing this, Alyssa shook her head and whispered, "It was magical."

"What?" Maggie strained to hear over the rest of the conversations in the room.

Alyssa laughed, closing her eyes. "I mean, it wasn't a date. It couldn't have been."

Janine had never seen a woman lie to herself so overtly.

"But we have a connection," Alyssa added simply. "Maybe it's as simple as that."

"It doesn't sound very simple," Janine said, tucking Alyssa's hair behind her ear.

Alyssa ignored her, gazing across the living room, where Francesca gestured a question: would you like dessert? And, laughing, Alyssa nodded, tying her hair up in a ponytail as her eyes glistened. Something was happening. She was no longer the same Alyssa she'd been several hours before.

And just like that, Janine thought, *I've lost her.*

But she wasn't even sure what she meant by that.

Chapter Thirteen

Alyssa announced the following morning that it was time to go to Mauricio Gionnocaro's house — they'd waited too long as it was. She then stuffed herself with a chocolate croissant, swallowed the single gulp of espresso in her cup, and hurried upstairs to shower. The stream of water came a split second later, interrupting the groggy thoughts in Janine's very slow morning mind.

"I guess we have an agenda for today," Maggie said.

"Chop chop," Janine said sarcastically.

After they dressed and headed out the door, Alyssa explained the reason for the renewed energy. Nico knew the curator at the Mauricio Gionnocaro House, and the curator had agreed to let the three of them into the back halls, where the "good stuff they don't let anyone see" was kept.

The Mauricio Gionnocaro House was probably three times as big as Teresa's villa, with ornate pillars along the front, a dramatic sculpture of a fallen angel battling a snake outside, and a grand hall with high ceilings upon first entrance. Upon the ceilings were paintings of dramatic scenes that seemed to depict the final days of earth, when heaven and hell battled till the end.

"Can you imagine wanting this in your house?" Maggie whispered.

"Not unless you want nightmares," Janine said.

At the front desk of the museum, Alyssa announced who they were and that the curator knew to expect them. A moment later, a very beautiful Italian woman with shiny, jet-black hair stepped out of the back hallway.

"Alyssa? Hello! My name is Barbara." Barbara, the curator, stuck her hand out for Alyssa to shake, and as she did, Alyssa looked crestfallen.

It occurred to Janine that Nico hadn't mentioned his curator friend being a very attractive woman. Alyssa was jealous— but she was also a professional. She wanted to get to the bottom of this, no matter what her personal feelings were.

"Good morning," Alyssa said, her voice wavering only slightly. "This is my mother, Janine, and my sister, Maggie."

"Welcome to the Mauricio Gionnocaro House," Barbara said, turning so that her glorious hair fell like a curtain around her shoulders and over her back. She then began to lead them through the house, toward the back halls, where the "secret collection" was presumably kept. "Nico tells me that you're on a quest to discover the truth about your family?"

"Something like that," Alyssa said.

"Well, I wouldn't be surprised if Mauricio Gionnocaro is some sort of connection," Barbara went on. "He was a fascinating man. Through the process of setting up this museum, we learned so much more about the secret society than ever before. Some people, those who clung to the secret society and its mysticisms, tried to get in the way of us learning more."

"What happened?" Maggie asked.

"A few of our founders were threatened," Barbara said. "A house was burned to the ground. A dog was kidnapped. Goodness, it was a mess. I wasn't around yet, but I heard the stories over and over again. You see, museum founders like to think of themselves as Indiana Jones types." She winked at Alyssa.

Barbara procured a very large, old key from her back pocket and opened a massive wooden door for them, behind which were the hidden records of the museum—that which they didn't let everyone parse through. At a table in the back of the large room was a very old woman at a sewing machine who glared at them behind half-moon glasses.

"That's Elena," Barbara explained quietly. "She's repairing the old curtains meant to hang in the upstairs rooms. She has to be here while you go through everything, just to keep an eye out. It's for legal reasons. I hope you don't mind?"

"We understand," Alyssa assured her.

Elena continued to glare at them from behind the sewing machine, as though, in coming into the back, they'd interrupted her concentration. Janine tried to smile, but it fell from her face.

"You'll find that everything is labeled," Barbara went on, taking them through the aisles of bookshelves and cabinets. "Photographs. Letters. Old diaries. Books. Trinkets. All of it was taken either from this house or the houses of Mauricio's contemporaries, of which there were many." Barbara paused, her eyes widening as though she'd just fully realized the depths of their task. "How long do you think you'll need?"

"Probably all day," Alyssa admitted, glancing at Janine and Maggie.

"We'll probably need breaks here and there," Janine said with a laugh.

"Of course," Barbara said. "There's a wonderful little lunch spot around the corner. Fabrizio's. We always pop in when we need something."

"Great tip. Thanks," Alyssa said, her eyes glinting—again with jealousy. Janine knew her well.

As Barbara breezed back out the large wooden door and closed it with a crunch behind her, Alyssa, Maggie, and Janine remained in the center of the shelves, blinking at one another nervously.

"Alyssa?" Maggie began. "What exactly are we looking for?"

Alyssa shrugged and took a step toward the nearest shelf. "Anything that connects the secret society to the Cacciapaglias. Anything that links that painting from the other museum to Mauricio or Teresa." She yanked open a cabinet drawer, glowering, then muttered, "Was she prettier than me?"

Both Maggie and Janine jumped into action.

"No way!" Maggie cried.

"No, honey," Janine assured her.

"And, come on. We saw how Nico looked at you yesterday," Maggie hurried to add. "He got you into the back room of the museum! It just so happens that she works here. It's a coincidence. That's all."

"They've probably been friends since they were kids," Janine tried. "It seems like everyone's known each other their entire lives here."

Alyssa wrinkled her nose, muttering, "I don't know," before she dove into her drawer. With a shrug, Janine and Maggie followed her lead, falling into their own drawers of research.

Janine's particular drawer was filled with diaries from the Gionnocaro family— which wasn't exactly helpful, as they were written entirely in Italian. Out of curiosity, she parsed through them, amazed at the beautiful handwriting of the 1800s, a lost art. She made a mental note to write more things down.

Maggie was more intelligent in her search, directing herself toward the photographs and putting her head down. "Mom, you have to come see these."

Janine hurried around the corner to look at the family photographs Maggie pulled out. They were from the late 1800s, early 1900s, creepy in the way old photographs often were, as nobody ever smiled, not even the children. Entire families were lined up near the canals, picnicking in a nearby field, or seated in a parlor somewhere, scowling at whoever had decided to take their photograph.

"Good idea on the photos," Alyssa said, joining them. "After all my research, I can pick out a few Italian phrases here and there, but I'm not quick. This is easier."

For the following two hours, the three Potter girls kept up their search as Elena, the seamstress, scowled at them from the back of the room. It wasn't till Janine thought she might fall over from hunger that Alyssa squealed in recognition.

She'd found something.

Maggie and Janine encircled her, peering down at a photograph of a pre-teenage girl. The photograph wasn't like the others, as it was still in a frame, the glass shattered over the feet of the girl.

"Look!" Alyssa cried, pointing to the calligraphy in the corner. "It says Teresa Cacciapaglia! Tell me it doesn't!"

Janine and Maggie squinted at the tiny, tiny writing and shook their heads in disbelief.

"I think you're right," Maggie whispered.

"Look at what she's wearing," Alyssa continued excitedly. "This crest hanging from her neck is in many, many other photographs and paintings, and, according to my research, it was the crest of the secret society. Which probably means that Teresa's father was somehow involved!"

Maggie lowered her voice. "I think you should take the photograph."

Alyssa gave her a look of shock. "Maggie! What's gotten into you!"

"Come on. She's our grandmother. Nobody has looked at that photograph in years," Maggie went on, showing a rare bit of rebellion.

Alyssa glanced back toward Elena, who'd become very focused on her sewing, her eyebrows furrowed.

Impatient, Maggie suddenly took the photograph, unlatched the back of the frame, and painstakingly removed it so that she could easily slip the photograph out. But as she did that, something cold and hard dropped from the back of the frame and smacked against the ground. Immediately, Elena raised her head and scowled at them, saying something in Italian.

"Sorry!" Alyssa piped up. "I dropped my phone." Alyssa then knelt gently, pretending to fetch her phone, and raised it up to show Elena.

At least for now, Elena was satisfied.

But meanwhile, Janine investigated what had actually fallen from the back of the frame. It had skidded across the floor, headed for the large wooden door that separated the archives from the public museum.

It was a small iron key.

Janine slipped the key into her pocket, her heart pattering wildly, as Alyssa slipped the photograph of Teresa into her purse and returned the frame to its position in the archives. So as not to make Elena suspect anything, Alyssa, Maggie, and Janine continued to search through the archives for a little while before they said goodbye to first Elena, then to Barbara outside.

"Did you find anything?" Barbara asked.

"We didn't, no," Alyssa said with a shrug.

"That's too bad," Barbara said. "Let me know if I can help you in some way. That society is fascinating. I'm sure there are ties to your grandmother."

Alyssa smiled. "Thank you so much, Barbara. Ciao."

Immediately after they left the museum, Alyssa's smile slid off her face. "She's just too beautiful," she muttered to Maggie and Janine. "And I'm pregnant!"

Janine sighed and wrapped her arm around Alyssa's shoulders. "All right. I think it's about time we had lunch. Blood sugar's getting low around here."

Alyssa rolled her eyes again but didn't resist.

"I'm starving," Maggie said.

But they didn't go to Fabrizio's. They knew to get as far away from the Mauricio Gionnocaro House as they could, as they'd stolen not one but two items from the archives, and they made their way back to the Grand Canal, where they dined at a pizza restaurant— eggplant with mozzarella, sausage with olives, and a truffle pizza that nearly destroyed them. The pizzas were small, allowing them each a couple of pieces of all three, their fingers shining with grease.

"So. You got it?" Alyssa locked eyes with her mother.

Janine nodded. "I did."

"But what could it be for?" Alyssa demanded.

"I have no idea," Janine said.

"It has to be the next clue, right?" Alyssa asked.

"It feels like a dead end," Maggie said, wiping her hands on her napkin. "But I love the photograph of Teresa. And it's fascinating to learn all about this society. Maybe that's enough?" She paused to swallow another bite of pizza, then added, "It's not like we need that villa or whatever money she left us, you know?"

But Janine knew that, for Alyssa, the scavenger hunt had never been about the money. It had always been about the thrill of the chase, the incredible opportunity to get to know their grandmother, even in death.

"We must have missed something," Alyssa said. "I just don't know what it is."

Chapter Fourteen

The flight to Venice was exhilarating. Nancy hadn't traveled internationally in ages, and she felt her soul buzzing, her laughter flowing easily, especially as the stewardess refilled her wine glass and brought her extra helpings of desserts. Beside her, Kostos seemed at-ease, entirely unlike a man who apparently got so nervous on airplanes. Frequently throughout the flight, he touched her hand, teased her, or tucked her hair behind her ear. Nancy felt doted on. She felt young and free.

After the flight touched down, Nancy waited at baggage claim as Kostos grabbed them coffees at a nearby kiosk. This pleased Nancy a great deal, feeling that she had a partner again. She'd forgotten what it meant for someone else to pick up the slack of her life.

Kostos hailed a taxi for them, and he heaved their suitcases into the back and greeted the driver in quick Italian. Together, the driver and Kostos had an elaborate and happy conversation all the way to the Grand Canal, where, apparently, they had to get out, as normal vehicles couldn't continue.

"Cars can't drive on water yet, unfortunately," Kostos joked as he removed their suitcases, then took Nancy's hand as they walked toward the edge of the dock. "Now, we have two options. We either take a water taxi or..." He nodded toward a classic gondola, where a man in a striped t-shirt and a hat rowed a beautiful couple along the water, singing as they went.

"Oh, it must cost an arm and a leg," Nancy said, her heart lifting.

"Don't you worry about that," Kostos told her, guiding her toward the gondola line, in which they stood for no more than five minutes before they were served. In Italian, Kostos explained where they were headed— Teresa's villa, but that they wanted a grand tour beforehand. The rower nodded, helped them into the boat, and then began to sing, his vibrato soaring across the ancient city. As Nancy sat in the creaking boat, her hands clasped around one of Kostos', she felt like a princess, a woman in a novel whose life was about to change forever. She'd felt similarly when she'd met Neal and fallen into his orbit. Still, she had to admit, Kostos was just that extra touch of magical, perhaps because he was so worldly.

"Does it look any different from the last time you were here?" Nancy asked.

"Not at all," Kostos said. "It's bizarre, as though it's stuck back in time."

"I don't think Venice should come into the twenty-first century," Nancy said. "It's like an old painting."

"It's a living, breathing painting," Kostos agreed.

After a forty-five-minute glide down the numerous canals, the gondola took them all the way to the same villa

Nancy had now seen in innumerable photographs from Janine, Maggie, and Alyssa. She would have recognized it anywhere. And just as the gondola creaked against the docks, Nancy heard, "Grandma!" cried out from the villa window. It was a delicious sound in such a foreign place.

"I think you're being called," Kostos teased, leaping from the boat to take Nancy's hand and help her out. Meanwhile, the gondola rower retrieved their suitcases and stacked them evenly on dry land. Kostos paid him handsomely, a tip that Nancy fully respected, then turned as Alyssa, Maggie, and Janine piled out of the house, all smiles. Alyssa and Maggie looked even more pregnant than ever, yet shining and happy, probably from all the wonderful food and sunshine.

One after another, Nancy hugged her Potter girls and made introductions. Kostos was charming as ever with them, complimenting the exterior of the villa and thanking them continually for allowing him to stay the night.

"Nancy knows how much I hate to fly," he explained as they entered the villa. "But I hardly even thought about it up there."

"That's wonderful," Janine said, giving Nancy a smile that meant a lot of different things— curiosity, happiness, confusion. "You spent the summer on Martha's Vineyard?"

"I was all alone there," Kostos affirmed. "Spending all these nights by myself. And then, suddenly, I met Nancy, and everything changed."

"She's pretty special," Janine agreed. "We've missed her."

Janine helped Kostos and Nancy bring their suitcases upstairs to two separate guest bedrooms and then gave them a brief tour of the house, finishing in the kitchen, where Alyssa and Maggie had made lemonade and espresso. They'd also purchased a variety of croissants and pastries, a divine first treat for the new arrivals.

"And we have something special planned for tonight!" Maggie added. "We hired a chef to come to the house to cook something spectacular."

"We know you'll be tired later," Alyssa explained. "And it's so nice to dine in this big, beautiful house. I love feeling like we're living the way Teresa did."

"I hope you didn't do all this on our account," Nancy said, although, of course, they had.

"Grandma, we're over the moon that you're here!" Alyssa said. "I've been lost in this scavenger hunt, basically going out of my mind."

Beside her, Maggie nodded. "It's been intense."

"Your grandmother was telling me about that," Kostos said as he sat at the kitchen table, eyeing the pastries. "How is it going?"

"We hit a dead end a couple of days ago," Alyssa explained sadly.

"And we're thinking about telling Teresa's lawyer that we're done," Maggie said.

Janine sighed and leaned against the counter. "It was really fun at the beginning."

"And we've learned a lot," Alyssa insisted.

"Alyssa's basically turned into a Venice historian," Maggie added.

Alyssa shrugged, her eyes glinting with pride. "I don't know about that."

Together, they feasted on pastries until Kostos admitted he needed to lie down for a little while, and Nancy agreed that sounded like a good plan. Up in her bedroom alone, she sat on the edge of the bed, thinking about Kostos on the other side of the wall, wondering if he was thinking about her, too. And when she finally drifted off into a nap that lasted the rest of the afternoon, she dreamed of him.

When Nancy awoke, there was noise coming from downstairs— Italian language, banging doors, Alyssa's laughter. Rubbing her eyes, Nancy got up and wandered to the mirror in the corner, where she did the best she could with a bit of makeup and concealer— all that could be done to freshen up her face, then headed downstairs to see what the fuss was about.

Maggie and Janine were in the living room, laughing together, as more and more bangs and raps came from the kitchen.

"What's happening down here? Is this place haunted?" Nancy asked.

"Practically," Janine said. "But you're not hearing the ghosts right now. That's just the chef prepping. He's got Alyssa in there, doing what she can with a big, flashy knife."

"Are they hacking the cabinets to bits?"

"I hope not," Janine said.

Nancy tip-toed to the doorway of the kitchen to watch as an Italian chef who looked to be in his fifties showed Alyssa how to use a knife over an onion, laughing when she didn't get it exactly right. He then turned to stir a pot on the stove and bang a skillet around as the peppers inside of it sizzled. Apparently, his version of cooking was percussive and expressive. Nancy had never seen anything like it before. Maybe it was the Italian way?

"Hi, Grandma!" Alyssa spotted her out of the corner of her eye. "Rico is showing me the ropes. Maybe I'll get the hang of Italian cooking before we head back to Martha's Vineyard."

"Oh, Martha's Vineyard! I hear it is the most beautiful place in the world," Rico said with a sigh.

"I don't know. Venice might be number one," Nancy said, smiling.

"That's sacrilegious, Grandma," Alyssa teased.

Nancy laughed. "Forgive me. I've never spoken ill of Martha's Vineyard before. What's for dinner?"

Rico spoke poetically about his five-course meal— the salad, the pasta, the fish, the meat, and the dessert, along with the fine Italian wines from the most intoxicating regions, which Nancy couldn't wait to try.

"This is an appropriate pre-dinner wine if you'd like a glass," Rico said, spinning the glass in his hands to show off a label of a tree, its limbs spread out beneath an inky-black sky peppered with stars.

"Very much so," Nancy said.

"Count me in!" Janine called from the next room.

By the time wines were poured for Janine and Nancy and lemonades were fixed up for Maggie and Alyssa, Rico had had enough of Alyssa in the kitchen.

"It's time for me to take over," he explained, swatting her out to join the rest of them in the living room.

Alyssa laughed and bounced onto the couch beside Nancy, cuddling against her. "Grandma, I'm so glad you're here."

Nancy's heart swelled.

"And this man you've brought!" Alyssa continued, lowering her voice slightly. "He's really something."

Nancy's cheeks burned with embarrassment as both Maggie and Janine leaned toward her, captivated and eager for gossip.

"It's been a whirlwind," Nancy said timidly. "It doesn't always feel like real life."

"It never does in the moment," Janine agreed.

"Alyssa's in one of those whirlwinds right now, too," Maggie teased.

Alyssa reached across the coffee table and swatted Maggie playfully.

"Yes! The Italian. Have you seen him again?" Nancy asked, having heard all about Nico.

"She went out for coffee with him this morning before he went to work," Maggie said, batting her eyelashes.

"We're just friends," Alyssa insisted.

Maggie gave Nancy a pointed look. "She keeps talking about their 'incredible connection.'" Maggie waved her fingers in air quotes.

Nancy beamed, knowing it had been a very long time since Alyssa had sensed a deeper connection with someone.

"Not to change the subject," Alyssa interjected, although that was clearly her plan, "but Hunter wrote me today and sent photographs of Lucy! Look." Alyssa turned her phone toward Nancy, who swiped through photo after photo of little Lucy (who, admittedly, looked much bigger than she had only a few weeks ago). In several, she rode a carousel as Hunter stood next to her horse and held onto her to ensure she didn't fall.

"They look happy," Nancy breathed. "Both of them."

Alyssa's eyes glinted.

"I sobbed when she showed them to me," Maggie admitted.

"But we're just so happy our girl is okay," Janine added.

Not long before dinner, Kostos emerged from

upstairs, looking well-rested, his eyes fresh. He kissed Nancy on the cheek and greeted the others joyously as Rico gathered them up and deposited them in the "formal" dining room, where they hadn't dined yet. The table had been set with immaculate china, presumably Teresa's, and the three wine glasses for non-pregnant people had already been filled with the wine Rico had deemed appropriate for this particular course. Nancy sat between Alyssa and Kostos, across from Maggie and Janine, as Rico served them the first course: stuffed artichokes that shimmered with butter. Just before they tucked in, Kostos raised his glass, saying, "To new friends and new adventures." And the rest of them agreed.

A worthy cook in her own right, Nancy was floored by this meal. Every morsel was divine, an explosion of flavor across her tongue, and every course defeated the previous as the best in the mix. Occasionally, they forgot to speak to one another, as they were entranced with their meal, lost in it.

But, during the brief pause between the fourth course and their dessert, Alyssa spoke about this and that, her hands flying over the table as though she'd become even more Italian since they'd gotten there. And then, abruptly, she stopped speaking, and her jaw hung open as she stared at something across the dining room.

"Alyssa? Are you all right?" At first, Nancy thought maybe she was choking, that she couldn't breathe.

Alyssa popped up from the table and wandered around it, gaping at something on the far wall.

"What's wrong?" Maggie followed her lead, walking alongside her until they reached an ornate cabinet, one meant for display rather than proper storage. It stood on the far end of the dining room, featuring some of the most gorgeous china Nancy had ever seen— probably worth much more than the beautiful china they currently ate on. It was probably hundreds of years old.

"Look at this," Alyssa said, pointing at a crest at the very top of the cabinet, beneath which was a keyhole. "It's the secret society's crest."

Beside her, Kostos abruptly stood from his seat, his hand around his neck. "Does this have something to do with your scavenger hunt?"

Maggie turned to nod. "We found a photograph of our grandmother wearing this crest. Behind that photograph was a key."

Alyssa pulled a necklace out from beneath her dress, on which hung a very old, ornate key. She then whipped the necklace from her neck, placed the key in the keyhole, and turned slowly. Everyone in the dining room watched, captivated, as the cabinet opened to reveal a small, ornate box.

"Oh my gosh!" Janine cried.

Alyssa's hands shook as she removed the box from the cabinet and carried it toward the dining room table. From the kitchen came the sound of Rico announcing, "Five minutes till dessert! Prepare your palates!" Nobody responded.

"This is it," Alyssa breathed. "The next clue."

"Or maybe it's the final one?" Janine suggested, hopefully.

Slowly, Alyssa removed the top of the box. In the box was a folded-up map, incredibly old, an antique, which she unfurled very gently. Upon the map, someone had drawn driving instructions, directly from outside of Venice, to the countryside outside of Florence, where there was a dramatic X in black ink.

"It's like a treasure map!" Nancy said.

"There's something else," Alyssa said, reaching for another folded-up piece of ancient paper. Again, she unfolded it to reveal blueprints for what looked like an enormous villa— four stories, sprawling grounds and gardens, a ballroom, three kitchens, and twenty-two guest bedrooms. It was captivating.

"Look at what it's called," Maggie whispered.

"Paradiso Terrestre!" Alyssa cried, her eyes widening as she turned to Nancy to explain. "That was the painting we saw in the Gallerie dell'Accademia!"

"This house must have been built where that X is on the map," Janine said.

"And it must have belonged to Teresa," Alyssa breathed. "We have to go there. We have to see it! It's a part of our inheritance. I know it."

Chapter Fifteen

Janine and Nancy went to the pastry shop the following morning to get everyone breakfast. Janine couldn't help but watch her mother's face as they breezed through the city, taking it all in as they went, her eyes alight and her smile never fading. When they reached the bakery, Janine impressed Nancy by ordering in Italian, then shrugged and said, "We've been here long enough for me to figure that out. But I can't begin to have a real conversation."

In fact, everything about the morning felt exquisite and completely gorgeous, until they walked through the front door of the villa and heard Alyssa sobbing.

"Alyssa?" Janine hurried through the foyer and ducked into the kitchen to find Alyssa at the counter, her hands over her eyes as her shoulders shook.

"They're gone. They're gone," she muttered over and over again, at a loss.

Janine and Nancy looked at one another with confusion.

"Who's gone, honey?" Janine asked.

"The blueprints! And the map." Alyssa threw her hands down and glared at them. "Did you leave the front door open? Did someone come in?"

Janine was flustered. "I'm sure you just put them somewhere else?"

"I put them with the Italian books from the library," Alyssa said.

There was a creak on the staircase, and a moment later, Maggie appeared, looking stricken.

"What's going on? I heard screaming."

Alyssa explained the situation: the lost map and blueprints, the assumption that someone had entered the house when Janine and Nancy had gone out for breakfast, and now, the fear: "Whoever took them is on their way to the house right now. Maybe there's something there. A historical document, or something the secret society wants to hide, or some kind of treasure?" Alyssa made a fist. "It means that someone was watching us. Someone wanted us to lead them to the next clue." Her face was stony. "Maybe it was Rico? He was here last night, watching us."

"He was so into his cooking," Janine interjected. "I don't think he had any idea what we were up to. He was angry when we weren't seated in time for dessert."

Alyssa's nose twitched. "Maybe it was Nico? I texted him about finding the map!"

"He wouldn't have broken into the house, would he have?" Maggie demanded.

"I don't know! He's a stranger!" Alyssa cried. "Gosh, I should have known. I mean, I'm pregnant! He would never date a pregnant woman. What kind of idiot am I? Oh no! Barbara must know that we took the key!"

"Don't jump to any conclusions," Janine urged. "Why

don't you sit down? Breathe for a second? We can figure this out."

But over the course of the next hour, it proved very difficult to calm Alyssa down. She'd hung her hopes and dreams upon this map and the blueprints and had probably spent the entire night dreaming about what awaited them there.

"I can't believe I didn't even take a photograph of the map," Alyssa muttered. "Nor of the blueprints. I feel like the biggest fool."

"You couldn't have known someone would take it!" Janine said, still trying to shove away her own heebie-jeebies— as her fear would only exacerbate theirs. Ultimately, if someone really had stolen from them, they probably had been watching them. Which, to Janine, meant one thing: "I think it's about time we head back to Martha's Vineyard, anyway. We should at least get out of Venice. I heard Capri's nice. We could get a house down there for a week, enjoy the sun for a while, and fly home?"

Alyssa looked unconvinced, as though she wanted to stand at the front door of the villa, glaring at passers-by until they confessed to their thieving. "Maybe I'll call Nico and see what's up. If he can't see me today, I'll know it's because he drove to Florence!"

Nancy tugged at her white curls, clearly at a loss. Janine reached for her hand, saying, "I'm sorry this is all happening right after you arrived."

"Oh, darlings! It's not your fault," Nancy assured them.

"I think we should get out of the house," Maggie suggested. "Maybe go to another museum? Eat lunch?"

Alyssa grumbled incoherently, lost in thought.

"It's not a bad idea," Janine said. "Until we decide what to do next."

"We could call the police," Alyssa suggested.

"And tell them what?" Maggie tried. "I mean, it seems like nobody knows that map or the blueprints exist in the first place. So, I can't imagine how the police would track them down."

Alyssa's chin quivered, but she didn't refute what Maggie said. "Maybe we can drive to approximately where the X on the map was?"

"We can't circle Florence all day," Maggie said with a sigh.

For a moment, they were quiet, the sorrow of this event pressing down upon them like a rain-filled cloud.

"Is Kostos still leaving today?" Janine asked her mother, tilting her head.

"Later this afternoon," Nancy offered. "Maybe he'd like a last lunch with everyone before he heads out. I'll go wake him up. I'm sure the jet lag has knocked him over."

Nancy disappeared up the staircase, leaving Alyssa, Maggie, and Janine alone in the living room. Partially, Janine had to admit she was glad the entire scavenger hunt was over and that they could move on with their lives. But she hated to see the disappointment in Alyssa's eyes.

"I can't even begin to call Nico to see if he did it," Alyssa said. "It hurts too much."

But suddenly, from upstairs, Nancy let out a horrific scream.

Janine burst to her feet and rushed up the staircase, moving far quicker than her pregnant daughters, unsure what awaited her— yet imagining horrific things, things she didn't want to verbalize. When she reached the guest bedroom where Kostos had been sleeping, she found Nancy seated on a mussed-up bed. The rest of the room was empty. Kostos' suitcase was gone.

Nancy looked stricken, her cheeks blotchy.

"Mom? Where's Kostos?"

Nancy's eyes were hollow. "I don't know."

Janine felt stiff with disbelief. In the back of her mind, she played over the events of yesterday, the conversations they'd had with Kostos, the way he'd made all of the women laugh. It had seemed effortless to him.

A moment later, Maggie and Alyssa appeared in the guest bedroom, equally confused.

"Grandma? Are you okay?" Alyssa asked.

"Kostos isn't here," Nancy said, her voice breaking. After a dramatic pause, she added, "He must have realized he didn't have feelings for me after all."

"So, he left without saying goodbye?" Janine demanded, her tone dark.

"What a baby," Maggie said. "I thought only younger guys got away with ghosting."

But Alyssa looked even more stricken than before. "Grandma, do you think Kostos took the map and blueprints?"

Nancy stuttered. "What? Why would he do that?"

"Call him," Maggie said. "Maybe it's just a misunderstanding. Maybe he's out getting breakfast, or..."

"Maggie, his suitcase is gone," Alyssa said firmly.

Nancy searched her pocket for her phone and called Kostos. Her chest did not rise as though she held her breath with fear. After six rings, he didn't answer. When she called again, it went straight to voicemail.

"He blocked you!" Alyssa cried.

Nancy blinked at Alyssa, clearly broken-hearted.

Janine's heart went out to her mother. She hated seeing her so defeated, cowering under the weight of a horrific man's decisions.

"When did you meet Kostos, Grandma?" Alyssa asked, sitting next to Nancy on the bed.

Nancy stuttered. "I told you. I met him…"

"The day we left," Janine answered, her heart pumping.

"It's just a coincidence," Nancy said.

"But what if it isn't a coincidence?" Alyssa suggested. "What if he targeted you to get close to us? What if he knew…"

"But I was the one who told him about Teresa and the scavenger hunt," Nancy said.

"Was he especially curious about it?" Maggie asked.

"Everyone was!" Nancy said. "It was weird and interesting. It was all anyone wanted to talk about."

The room fell silent. Alyssa had her arm around her grandmother, holding her as she shook, and Maggie and Janine exchanged glances, both of them eager to save the day, yet unsure how.

"Why don't we wait a little bit longer?" Janine said. "If Kostos doesn't reveal himself by this afternoon, we'll know we have a problem. And we'll call the police."

Nobody had another idea, so they went with hers. As they returned downstairs wordlessly, Janine marveled that, although she was an adult, she was often struck with the feeling that she had no idea what to do, where to go, or what the proper solution was. Maybe everyone felt that way.

As they waited for a sign from Kostos, Alyssa called Nico, who came over immediately, both proving himself not to be the thief and proving himself loyal to Alyssa. As they spoke in the dining room, Janine stepped into the hallway to call Henry and explain what had happened. Henry was captivated.

"Kostos? Really? That Greek guy?" he stuttered.

"You met him. Did you get any sense he was trying to swindle my mother?"

"I don't know," he said. "Gosh, Janine. I wish I was there with you. This is freaking me out."

Janine closed her eyes, imagining herself safe within the arms of this man, back home in the familiar Martha's Vineyard sunlight.

"I think you should call the police, just in case," Henry said. "And maybe, if they can't find Kostos, you should go to a hotel tonight, just to be safe."

Janine thanked him, told him she loved him, and then returned to her family, who, after a conversation with Nico, had decided the same thing. It was time to call the cops.

Two police officers arrived at the villa within the hour. One of them, Vio, spoke much better English than his partner, Arturo, so Vio did most of the talking. After they explained to them what they knew, along with the connection to the secret society, Vio explained everything to Arturo, who made several phone calls to the Venice police station, followed by the Florence police station. When he returned to the living room, he was pale as snow.

Beside her, Nancy gripped Janine's hand hard, sensing something very wrong.

In English, Vio explained what Arturo had just learned on the phone.

"We've tracked down your friend, the Greek man."

Nancy sniffed with shock. "Is he all right?"

"It depends on the definition of 'all right,' I suppose. He's in custody in Florence," Vio said.

"What!" Alyssa and Maggie cried out.

Vio nodded. "The story is he came into a bar outside of Florence, drank himself to drunkenness, and began to rave and scream like a madman. He was very angry." Vio swallowed nervously. "The police in Florence say they have the map and the blueprints you're talking about. The Greek man had them when he was arrested."

"Oh my gosh," Nancy whispered. Janine could just feel the sinking of her mother's heart, coming to terms with the criminality of the man she'd fallen for.

"The police in Florence know about the villa," Vio went on. "The one from the map. The one in the blueprints."

"They do?" Alyssa asked, leaning forward, hungry for knowledge.

"It was destroyed two years ago," Vio went on. "It was filled with black mold. Nobody could go inside."

Immediately, Alyssa's face fell. Even Janine felt heavy with this news, as though all the air had been sucked out of the room.

"In any case, it seems that the Greek man drove to where the villa was supposed to be, went crazy looking through what's left of it, and even dug for a while before he retreated to this bar, dirty and out of his mind, got himself very drunk, and was then arrested," Vio went on. "I'm very sorry to tell you this." He paused for a moment, glancing at Arturo. "Would you like to file a police report?"

"We need to be sure Kostos won't come back here," Janine said simply.

"We'll have the Florence officers warn him about that," Vio said. "It's all we can do at this stage."

"Could you learn more about who this man actually is?" Janine breathed. "He seems to have stalked my mother back in Martha's Vineyard to get close to us."

"We can look into that, ma'am. I imagine his name isn't what he says it is," Vio said.

After Vio and Arturo left, and Nico admitted he had to head to the museum, Janine, Alyssa, Maggie, and Nancy sat listlessly in the shadows of the living room, Nancy with Kleenex wadded up in her fist, sniffing every few minutes. The grandfather clock was especially loud, ticking them forward through time.

"I'm so, so sorry, girls," Nancy muttered. "I can't believe I endangered you. I brought that horrible man into this house."

Janine wrapped her arms around her mother. "The only word I keep thinking is 'relief.' He didn't hurt us. He didn't demand the map. We found it the first night he was here, which probably saved us." Janine eyed Alyssa from across the room to add, "You saved us, Alyssa. You and your quick wits."

But Alyssa was devastated and disappointed. Although she didn't say it aloud, Janine knew she'd hung her hopes on whatever was in that villa. But whatever it was, it had been destroyed.

There was nothing else to be done, nothing to be said. Without knowing it, they'd gotten themselves involved in a real-life thriller. And now, they had to pick up the pieces and head home without the "treasure" they'd sought.

Chapter Sixteen

It did not take the Florence police force long to figure out who Kostos really was. In fact, by the following afternoon, Vio and Arturo were back in Teresa's villa, explaining to Janine and Nancy what they'd learned.

Apparently, Kostos went by many names— all of them Greek-sounding, all of them mystical and alluring. He'd operated as a con artist for many years, normally preying on women of a certain age, getting close to them to get to their money. It was probable that he'd learned of Teresa's money and will through the grapevine, as rumors about her "scavenger hunt" had circulated even before her death. Probably, her lawyer had told someone, who'd told someone else, who'd told someone else. Outside of the secret society, Italians were terrible at keeping secrets.

"The fact that he went to Martha's Vineyard to find you means that he really thought this particular 'treasure' was something special," Vio explained.

"You should have seen the house he rented," Nancy breathed. "It was extraordinary."

"He's made a killing on these other scams," Vio said. "I imagine he could afford that."

After Vio and Arturo again apologized, leaving Janine and Nancy alone in the living room, Nancy dropped back against the cushion of the couch and stared at the ceiling. "I still feel like a fool," she breathed.

"But you shouldn't."

Nancy gave Janine a side-eyed look. "He called me a woman of a certain age."

Janine laughed. "We're all women of certain ages. I don't even know what he means by that."

Nancy laced her fingers through Janine's. "Gosh, I'm so glad I never..." She trailed off.

"You never did?"

"No."

Janine nodded, grateful for that, as well. Had Nancy slept with Kostos, she knew Nancy's shame would have been amplified.

"I thought I was too old to let men manipulate me like that," Nancy said. "I thought I'd moved on to the next phase of my life. And oh, Janine. You should have heard the stuff he said to me about Neal. He said all the right things."

"I'm sure he did." Janine sighed.

"Tell me I'm not an idiot."

"You're not an idiot in the slightest."

Maggie appeared at the bottom of the staircase, having been upstairs, taking a nap. "Did I hear the cops again?"

"They were here," Janine said, explaining what they'd come to say. Maggie wrinkled her nose.

"I'm so sorry, Grandma."

Alyssa was, yet again, out with Nico— wandering through alleyways, sailing through canals, or eating delectable food. Janine sensed that Alyssa was trying to lap up the last bit of their dreamy days in Italy and forget what had happened with Kostos. Nico was a welcome distraction.

"What do you say we fly home in a few days?" Janine asked Maggie. "Grandma and I were just looking at flights."

Maggie puffed out her cheeks and sat across from them in the living room. "I feel way more pregnant than I did when we first got here. I don't know how Alyssa is moving around so well. I want to go back to the Vineyard and sleep till the baby comes."

"That makes sense," Janine said.

"Alyssa will be sad to leave her Italian boyfriend," Nancy said sadly.

Everyone was quiet for a moment, recognizing the weight of what Alyssa was giving up. This was the first man worthy of Alyssa's love. He just happened to live thousands of miles away.

"She'll find someone else," Maggie said softly, speaking to the floor. "I did, even when I thought I never would."

"She has you and the babies," Nancy offered. "I'm sure that's enough love to go around for now." But she didn't sound like she was sure.

* * *

For the next several days, Janine didn't see much of Alyssa. She swept in and out of the Italian villa, headed to meet Nico, to hang out with his friends, or to go on brief sailing expeditions, each time exploring further into the turquoise blue. Janine, Nancy, and Maggie missed her, of course, and would have loved to have her with them— but they understood her needs. Maggie's pregnancy had taken a turn, and she required much more sleep than normal, frequently opting out of Janine and Nancy's Venice explorations or museum visits. Now that September was here, the city had shifted, and autumn could be felt with each breath, lingering at the edge of the heat.

"Isn't it interesting? We came all this way to distract the girls from missing Lucy," Janine reminded Nancy. "And now, back home, we'll need to find a way to distract Alyssa from missing Nico."

"It's a blessing and a curse to have so much love," Nancy agreed, her voice slightly brighter than it had been immediately after Kostos' arrest. Janine strung her arm through her mother's, wandering there beside the Grand Canal, still as captivated as ever by its beauty.

Janine contacted Francesca, Eva, and Teresa's lawyer to explain what had happened. Teresa's lawyer asked, "Is this you giving up on Teresa's game?" And Janine said, "I believe so." To this, the lawyer said, "I'll make the appropriate arrangements after you've left. Everything that was meant to be yours will now go to charity."

Janine sensed this was the right way forward, anyway.

One day before their flight back to Martha's Vineyard, Alyssa and Maggie were in their bedrooms, packing, when there was a knock at the door. A shiver of fear raced up and down Janine's spine. She wasn't sure she wanted to answer it, fearing Kostos and his wrath. But when she did, she found Nico on the front stoop, gasping for breath. His face glistened with sweat.

"Is Alyssa here? She's not answering her phone."

"Yes? She's upstairs. Alyssa?" She stepped back to allow Nico to enter, and he stood in the foyer of the old house, staring at the staircase, until Alyssa walked down, holding her stomach.

"Nico! What are you doing here?" Alyssa's smile was enormous. "I just realized you called me fifteen times! Sorry, I didn't have my sound on."

Nico strung his fingers through his hair. "It's okay! It is." He swallowed. "I have something to show you. To show all of you, if you're willing to come back to the Mauricio Gionnocaro House."

"The what house?" Nancy asked.

"What is it?" Alyssa demanded, her tone shifting. "What did you find?"

But Nico shook his head. "It's easier to show you."

Alyssa locked eyes with Janine, who nodded. "Let's go."

When they reached the Mauricio Gionnocaro House, the same museum employee, Nico's friend, Barbara, greeted them. This time, perhaps armed with her assured love for Nico, Alyssa didn't seem jealous at all. She even kissed Barbara twice on the cheek as though they'd become friends.

"Nico was texting me this morning about what happened," Barbara said. "And it triggered a memory! I knew you needed to see this."

Barbara led them again through the thick wooden door, behind which Elena continued to sew and sew at her machine, her brow furrowed. Janine pitied her, all alone in that room. Then again, maybe that's exactly where she wanted to be.

Toward the back of the room, near the thick, black curtains that protected the museum archives from direct sunlight, were racks and racks of paintings.

"They're unorganized," Barbara said, tugging at the top of her shirt. "Which freaks me out a bit." Quietly, she added, "In a museum, we're trained to organize, organize, organize. But when Paradiso Terrestre was destroyed a couple of years ago, we simply didn't have the time to organize everything they brought to the museum."

Janine's jaw dropped. Beside Alyssa, Nico's face glowed with pride.

"They brought things here from the villa?" Nancy asked.

"Of course," Barbara said. "That villa was designed by Mauricio himself, around the time he stole the actual painting— which, as you probably know, was returned by his daughter many years after his death. The villa was a known meeting place for the secret society."

Nobody knew what to say. Alyssa gaped at Barbara in disbelief.

"In any case, when Nico told me about your grandmother, I remembered something within the mess they brought us," Barbara said, reaching forward proudly to flip over the first painting in a stack. It was clear she'd brought it out of the chaos, front and center, so that she could do the big reveal like this— as though she were a magician.

The painting was of Teresa as a young woman, perhaps in her mid-twenties. In it, she sat at a mahogany desk in a black dress, a pen poised over a piece of paper, and her face was pale and unsmiling. Around her neck was the same crest she'd worn in the photograph of her as a pre-teen.

"What is she writing?" Janine whispered.

Barbara gestured toward the corner of the desk, where an envelope sat. "I was curious, so I already looked into it. That envelope is already addressed to the United States. And Nico tells me Teresa married an American man?"

"And had his child. Our father," Alyssa said softly.

"It's impossible to know, but maybe she's writing to her son," Barbara said.

"I'd like to think that," Maggie said. "Thank you."

Janine crossed her arms over her chest, studying the sorrow in Teresa's eyes. It was true that her age in the portrait dictated she'd already left her young son in the United States, that she'd already gone through so much loss, even in her mid-twenties. Janine's heart went out to her.

"Can I look at something? Something on the back?" Alyssa stepped forward, eyeing Barbara.

Barbara hurried up to help Alyssa turn the painting gently so that the back was facing them again. Alyssa's fingers fluttered gently along the edge of the painting, searching for something. There had been a key hidden behind the photograph. Why not also behind the painting?

"You think there's something hidden?" Barbara asked.

"It's our last clue," Alyssa said. "I have to make sure."

Barbara nodded and began to search as well, rubbing nails, feeling at the hard, old canvas that stretched along the back. Just when Janine wanted to suggest they give up, that the train ended here, Alyssa shrieked, "I think I found something!" And then, from between two nails that kept the canvas attached to the wood of the frame, she tugged out a folded-up piece of yellow paper. Yet again, Janine's jaw dropped. There was no end to Alyssa's brilliance.

Captivated, they watched as Alyssa unfolded the piece of paper, wordless, until she said, "It's a birth certificate for someone named Giovanni Cacciapaglia." Her voice wavered as she added, her eyes thick with tears, "His mother's name was Maria Cacciapaglia, and his father's name was Leonardo Serrano." Alyssa frowned, studying the certificate a moment more. "I don't know what some of these words mean." She passed it over to Nico.

Nico nodded as he read, looking very grave. "Maria died in childbirth. Leonardo was already dead when the baby arrived."

Janine pressed her hand to her chest. "Oh no. That's terrible."

Alyssa took the birth certificate back, frowning.

After a long silence, Maggie whispered, "But why did Teresa lead us here? What does this have to do with us?"

Alyssa blinked several times, studying the document, until her shoulders sagged. "It's Dad's birthday."

"What?" Janine demanded.

"On the birth certificate." Alyssa passed it over to Janine, who thought she might pass out. "Look."

Sure enough, the date Giovanni Cacciapaglia had been born was the very day Janine had celebrated Jack Potter's birth, year after year. But what did it mean? Why was this at the end of the scavenger hunt?

Alyssa closed her eyes. "Oh my gosh. Teresa wasn't his real mother. And his father wasn't his real father."

Janine's heart seized. "How can we be sure?"

"We have to go," Alyssa stuttered. With the birth

certificate still in her hand, she reached out to take Barbara's and shake it. "Thank you so much for your help, Barbara. Really. We couldn't have done this without you."

Barbara smiled confusedly. "You're so welcome. Let me know if you want to come back. I'm always happy to help one of Nico's friends. You know, we grew up together? He's like my brother."

Back outside, Janine, Maggie, Nancy, Alyssa, and Nico grabbed a table in the piazza and ordered a variety of sparkling waters, juices, and wines. Nobody knew what to say. But a few minutes after they received their drink orders, Eva arrived, her smile bright. Apparently, Alyssa had invited her without telling the others.

"Good afternoon! I heard a rumor you're heading out tomorrow," Eva said as she slipped a chair between Alyssa and Janine. "What a terrible thing. I hope you'll come back to visit soon."

Everyone at the table assured her they would; they couldn't stay away.

And then, Alyssa asked the million-dollar question. "Eva? Do you know who Maria Cacciapaglia is?"

Immediately, Eva's face was shadowed, sinister. "How do you know that name?"

"I can explain everything," Alyssa said. "Just tell us who she is."

Eva no longer looked pleased to be there. "She was my mother and Teresa's little sister, the black sheep of the family. She got involved in some horrible business with that society. Oh, goodness. I'll never forgive them for how they brainwashed her! Mind you, this was all long before I was born, but my mother never let me forget."

Janine's stomach twisted into knots. She hadn't expected this turn.

"What happened to her?" Alyssa breathed.

"She met a man in the society," Eva said. "And he was cruel and manipulative. The family never saw her again."

"But Teresa was in the society," Maggie interjected.

"Yes. And, well, it's true that Teresa got Maria involved," Eva whispered. "But Teresa never let it take over her life. Not like Maria did. I don't think Teresa ever forgave herself for Maria's disappearance."

Janine's eyes filled with tears. Slowly, Alyssa removed the birth certificate from her pocket and unfurled it in front of Eva, who blinked down at it, her eyes spinning with confusion.

"We know this is my father's birth certificate," Alyssa said, her voice catching. "Which means Maria was our grandmother, not Teresa. And Teresa took Giovanni as her own, went to the United States, and ultimately married our grandfather."

Eva was quiet for a long time, staring at the birth certificate— proof of a secret society's horrific attacks on a wonderful family. "Leonardo was the man who took Maria away from the family," she affirmed. "But I didn't know he died. I didn't know Maria died in childbirth. Oh, no. This cannot be." She placed her hand over her mouth.

"It's a lot to take in," Maggie said, wiping a tear from her own cheek.

Eva lifted her eyes toward Janine. "You're the only one who knew Jack's father. Why did he do it? Why did he adopt this Italian baby and call him Jack Potter?"

Janine's memories of Jack's father were ancient, filled with shadows and personal resentments. Constantly, she'd felt frightened of Jack's father's rage, his assurance that Janine wasn't enough for their family.

"He must have really loved Teresa," Janine offered finally. "I have no other explanation."

"But he cheated on her," Maggie pointed on.

Janine gave Maggie a pointed look. She wanted to translate that just because Rex had cheated on Maggie, and just because Jack had cheated on Janine, and just because so many people had wronged so many others across the centuries upon centuries of human relationships, that didn't mean there had never been love. It didn't negate the love that had come before, either.

"He loved his son," Janine said quietly. "He loved him more than I can possibly describe. When Jack lost his dad, well, he wasn't the same after that. Theirs was a bond that went beyond birth certificates. And gosh, this is messy. But for some reason, Teresa wanted Jack to know the truth. But he died not knowing."

Chapter Seventeen

Teresa's lawyer came over to the villa that night to congratulate them on completing the hunt. It did not feel joyful— but it did feel as though they'd accomplished something, which maybe had to be enough. The lawyer went on to explain just how little money Teresa had so late in her life and that her only reasonable offerings in terms of inheritances were located within that very villa, plus the villa itself. This wasn't entirely a surprise, especially when the lawyer explained the economy in Italy right now and the fact that families like the Cacciapaglias had wonderfully historical names but not a lot else.

It was Alyssa's idea to make the villa into a sort of museum. "If this secret society really had such an effect on Maria's life, then they probably conducted other evils. We should dedicate the museum to people like Maria, people who attempted to serve a power greater than themselves but got caught up in their game."

After a bit of digging, Nico suggested that when Teresa returned from the United States, she remained partially involved with the secret society. Rumors circulated that she was partially to blame for the secret society's downfall. "We can get to the bottom of that story. That's what your museum should be about," he said.

To this, Alyssa said, "You should be in charge of the museum, Nico. You have the researching skills and the background for it." She then turned toward Janine for back-up, and Janine nodded whole-heartedly, loving watching her daughter take charge like this.

Although it was suggested that they change their flights and head back to Martha's Vineyard in a few more days, Alyssa eventually was the one to call it. "I have to bite the bullet and say goodbye to Nico eventually. It might as well be tomorrow."

Before they headed to the airport the following morning, Nico met them at the villa, where he took Alyssa on a long walk through the canals.

"I can only imagine how romantic he is with her," Maggie said with a sad laugh as Janine gathered her suitcase and carried it downstairs for her, unwilling to let her pregnant daughters carry anything.

"You must be excited to see David," Janine said, turning as she set down the suitcase in the foyer.

"I am," Maggie said softly. "Are you excited to see Henry?"

"I can't wait."

On the couch, Nancy stared out the window at the beautiful, early-September morning, at the sunlight that glimmered on the canals so far from home. She'd come all the way to Italy with a potential lover, and she'd leave only with her family. Janine hoped she'd find a way through this.

Four hours out across the ocean, as they closed their

airplane window blinds against the splintering daylight, Alyssa burst into tears. Quietly, Maggie told her sister it would be all right, that she and Nico could keep in touch, and that all was not lost.

To this, Alyssa whispered, "I just realized how terrified I am of everything that comes next. I was hiding from my pregnancy and the childbirth and the baby coming, throwing myself into Teresa's game as a distraction. And now? Everything is crashing down." She tried to laugh, but it only made her cry more.

Maggie's voice was even softer now. "You don't have to stay with me and the babies. You really don't. You never agreed to that."

But Alyssa was adamant. "You're my everything, Maggie. I could never leave you and the babies."

Behind them, Janine's heart shattered over and over into a million pieces, until Nancy reached over and squeezed her hand. "It's going to be okay," she mouthed. Janine realized, then, that her cheeks were streaked with tears.

When the plane touched down in Boston, more than three weeks after their departure, almost every single member of their family met them at Arrivals. Elsa, Bruce, Mallory, Cole, Aria, Carmella, baby Georgia, David, and, of course, Henry waved their arms and covered them with hugs. After such a long flight, it was momentarily overwhelming. But the comfort of their love was grounding, like falling into bed after a long day.

Henry, especially, was a gorgeous sight to see. It was chillier in Boston, in the lower sixties, and he wore a ball cap and a button-down and wrapped his arms around Janine, kissing her on the forehead, then the cheek, then the lips.

"You've had a wild adventure, haven't you?" he breathed into her ear, and she shivered against him.

"After all that chaos, I think I'm ready to get married now," she told him, surprising herself.

Henry laughed. "That's music to my ears."

And in his car that evening, as the sunlight dimmed across the Atlantic, Janine held his hand and leaned her head against the car seat, listening to the soft rhythm of Henry's words as he talked about his documentary, about everything she'd missed when she'd been away, and of the upcoming autumn season, during which they could finally, finally rest after the chaos of the summer.

And, Janine thought now of Jack, of how, for a brief moment in time, years ago, she'd felt similarly safe with him. He'd been the son of two long-deceased Italians, the names of whom she'd only just learned. And maybe it was a tragedy that he'd never gotten to know that. But she had, and she would carry his story for him, whether he deserved it or not.

Chapter Eighteen

During the second week of September, the Athens, Greece authorities contacted Nancy. The number that flashed up on her cell phone was surprising, the country and area code nothing she recognized, but she answered it to hear a somber, precise-sounding Greek woman say, "Is this Nancy Remington?"

"It is."

"My name is Aphrodite, and I work in the Athens police department. I have some questions regarding someone we have in custody. Although his real name is Eli, you probably knew him as..."

"Kostos," Nancy finished, her throat tight. She sat in her office in the Katama Lodge, overlooking the beautiful bay that glistened beneath an eggshell blue sky. Athens felt like several dimensions away. "I'm happy to answer any questions you have."

Nancy was glad to learn through Aphrodite that Kostos was being tried on twelve counts of scamming. The women he'd encountered and stolen from over the years had come out of the woodwork, grateful to do whatever they could to ensure he never seduced and ruined anyone ever again.

"You got lucky," Aphrodite finished toward the end of their call. "He made a fortune off of lonely women across the world. You were his match, and you took him down."

"The treasure he was after never really existed. He was like Don Quixote, fighting a monster that wasn't there."

"Well said."

Nancy hung up the phone, sighed, and stretched her arms over her head. If she thought long and hard about the previous month of her life, she was apt to drive herself crazy. It was better to take each day as it came.

At six that evening, Nancy had another yoga class to teach, after which she planned to head back to the Remington House. With a few minutes to spare, she breezed past Janine's office to find her daughter leaning over her desk, her glasses pressed low over her nose as she read a patient's file. As Nancy studied her, hard at work, saving so many patients' lives, Nancy's heart swelled with love for her. Naturopathy was an under-appreciated corner of the medicinal world, but Nancy understood Janine's promise: she was enthusiastic with each patient, eager to listen, to accommodate their needs. She understood that everyone came from a different background and was armed with a different range of stories that ultimately influenced their health.

Janine sensed Nancy's gaze and lifted her eyes, smiling. "Are you spying on me?"

Nancy laughed. "Just waiting for you to finish. I didn't want to interrupt."

Janine set down her pen. "Okay."

"Will you be at home tonight for dinner? I was

thinking about making lasagna now that it's not so gosh-darn hot."

Janine hesitated.

"If you planned to be with Henry tonight, don't worry," Nancy hurried to add.

"I was just going to ask if I can invite him over," Janine said.

"Oh! Of course." Nancy laughed gently. "Henry's always welcome. I'll text Maggie that she should invite David, too."

"Did you see Alyssa before you left the house this morning?" Janine asked, her face marred with worry.

Alyssa had more-or-less holed up at the Remington House since their return from Venice. With her due date in November right around the corner, she'd taken to nesting, organizing a nursery for the baby, texting and calling Nico regarding the newly founded Teresa Cacciapaglia Museum, and insisting that she was "totally fine" when it came to all things Nico. "It was just a little fling. Not even a fling! We were basically just friends," she'd said. But there was a sorrow in Alyssa's eyes that made everyone walk on eggshells around her.

"I made her some breakfast," Nancy said. "But she wanted to eat in her room rather than at the table with me. I assume she wanted to call Nico about that diary he wants to put in the museum."

Janine sighed and rubbed her temples, as though she pushed off an incoming headache. "If my memory serves me correctly, seven months pregnant isn't the most comfortable feeling. I hope she's getting enough rest."

"She'll be okay. The museum is a worthy distraction from her heartache, I think," Nancy offered. "We just have to make sure she remembers how much she's loved."

Nancy padded upstairs to the yoga studio, beside which ten women were already lined up, their yoga mats under their arms, their ponytails swinging. Nancy greeted them quietly, unlocked the door, and turned on the lights as they flattened out their yoga mats and prepared for the next hour.

Just before Nancy asked them to quiet down, a familiar face appeared in the doorway.

"Stan?" Nancy's heart lifted, and she bounced toward the door with more enthusiasm than she'd felt since they'd gotten back.

Stan Ellis wore a pair of sweatpants and a black t-shirt, and he carried a yoga mat under his arm, just like the women in the class. Nancy remembered that he'd previously attended her yoga classes when he'd lived at the Lodge, which had resulted in less back pain and a better posture. She'd pestered him about coming back, but he never had until now.

"Your secretary said I can just book classes online whenever I want to," Stan told her, his voice wavering. "But I couldn't figure out how to work the dang website!"

Nancy laughed. "I can understand that. You should have told me, though. I would have booked you in earlier."

Stan stood nervously for a moment, blinking out across the room, now filled with women.

"Why don't you set up over there in the corner?" Nancy suggested. "We're about to get started."

"I'm not sure if I'm half as flexible as I was when I was coming all the time," Stan told her.

"I only ask for your best effort in this room," Nancy reminded him. "Nothing more, nothing less."

Stan saluted her. "Aye, aye, captain."

Nancy was grateful that, over the course of the next hour, she was able to seamlessly fall into her "yoga teacher" persona— and avoid all thoughts of handsome Stan in the corner of the room. Once, as she walked through the rows of students, adjusting their yoga stances here and there, she caught herself wanting to touch Stan's extended arm just to see what the muscle felt like. A shiver raced up and down her spine, and a voice echoed in her mind: *Don't be stupid, Nancy. You just fell for Kostos, and look how that turned out!*

Even still, another voice splintered through that one to say: *Stan is different. You know that.*

After the yoga class finished, the women thanked Nancy, rolled up their yoga mats, and returned to the hallway, chatting as they went. Only Stan took his time, his forehead glistening as he rolled up his mat very slowly. It had clearly been a difficult workout for him.

Nancy waited at the front of the class, her heart thudding as he approached. When he did, his smell made her woozy, and she remembered reading once, in a women's magazine, that you should like the way a man's sweat smells. It meant you were compatible. She'd thought that was so strange at the time.

"Great workout, Nancy," Stan said, stuttering slightly.

"Thanks for coming!"

"It was my pleasure. I'd heard you were in Italy for a while, and I was worried you weren't coming back," Stan said.

Nancy waved her hand. "I was just visiting my daughter and granddaughters. We all came back together."

"They moved back into that big, old place with you? You aren't all alone anymore?"

"No. Thank goodness. My granddaughters are getting more and more pregnant by the day, which means they need me all the more. That said, my daughter has been spending a great deal more time with her fiancé. I think they're going to get married officially next spring and probably move in together. Oh, but listen to me! I'm blabbering. What's new with you, Stan?"

"Nothing, as usual," Stan said. "Just living out my days in my little shack."

"I'm sure it's no shack, especially now that you've refurbished it." She knew Stan's ex-stepson, Tommy Gasbarro, had had a huge hand in building it back up since the hurricane. And then, acting braver than she had in years, she heard herself say, "Maybe you could show it to me sometime?"

Stan looked taken aback. "Really?"

Nancy raised her shoulders. "You're a good friend of mine, Stan. I'd love to see where you live."

Stan wasn't accustomed to the rest of the world looking at him as worthy, as anything but the man who'd killed Anna Sheridan. Nancy was bent on proving to him he was so much more than his mistakes— even if it took years of reminding him.

"What about tomorrow night?" Nancy heard herself ask.

Stan stuttered. "Tomorrow night works for me."

"Great," Nancy said. "You don't need to worry about cooking."

"I like to cook," Stan said, his tone firm. "Don't you worry about that."

That night, when Nancy pulled the lasagna from the

oven in the Remington House, she had a full kitchen. Maggie and David were at the kitchen table, with Maggie demanding David read several passages of a baby book she'd recently learned was the "best of the best in baby knowledge during the year 2023."

"Does that mean everything they knew in 2022 is now deemed incorrect?" Nancy asked as she slid the very hot lasagna onto the stovetop and waved her oven mitt through the steam.

Maggie glowered. "They have researchers working around the clock to learn everything there is to know about babies! It's up to new mothers to learn everything."

Janine was at the kitchen counter with Henry, drinking a glass of Malbec as Henry showed her a recent edit of a documentary he was making with Quentin Copperfield. Janine laughed at something on the screen, and Henry said, "Yeah, we didn't expect him to do that!" Nancy marveled at the ease with which they stood alongside one another, lost in their own world.

"Where's Alyssa? Is Carmella still here?" Nancy asked.

Suddenly, Alyssa breezed into the kitchen, her phone raised as she video-chatted with Nico all the way across the Atlantic. Since they'd officially hired him to start the Teresa Cacciapaglia Museum, he'd been hard at work, going through the numerous unused documents at the Mauricio Gionnocaro House, discussing appropriate ways of curation with more experienced museum employees, and hiring other museum historians to ensure he did everything correctly. Alyssa had had a hand in every step of the process; her eyes were fiery as she asked questions, provided suggestions, and demanded photographs of almost every new artifact he discovered.

"Alyssa! Dinner's ready," Nancy reminded her.

"I have to run, Nico," Alyssa said without missing a beat. "Isn't it one in the morning there, anyway?" She burst into love-filled giggles, then showered him with "Ciao! Ciao, Nico!" until they hung up.

For a moment, everyone in the kitchen was quiet as Alyssa swam in her own lovey-dovey thoughts.

"Oh! It looks delicious, Grandma!" She waddled over to the stovetop to peer down at the lasagna.

"And it's going to get cold if we don't eat it," Nancy said, swatting her gently with an oven mitt. "Carmella? Are you here, too?" She called it out through the echoing house.

Carmella was, in fact, there, which meant that three of the seven adults present for dinner were pregnant. The air over the dining room table was light and happy, shimmering with their blessings, and outside, an autumn wind blasted against the windows and rafters. And all the while, through everything she heard and everything she said, Nancy floated on a hopeful feeling that tomorrow, when she went to Stan's place, everything in her life would shift to a different gear. That finally, she would open her heart to the right man.

And maybe, she thought now, her days at the Remington House were numbered. It was the first time she'd thought that since she'd moved in with Neal all those years ago, yet now it seemed natural, organic. This house had never been hers, not really. And it sat better with her to pass it on to Maggie, Alyssa, and the babies—if they were open to that.

But the conversation for that would come later, she knew. Not now, when everything still existed in possibilities and summer fizzled out.

Chapter Nineteen

On the morning of November 7th, Janine returned home from staying over at Henry's, her bags ladened with dirty laundry from her many days away, her heart floaty from pretending to live with him permanently. She opened the front door to find Alyssa in the living room in a bright red dress (a bit more dressed up than she normally was around the house), chatting on her computer to none other than her "not boyfriend," Nico, all the way in Italy. Alyssa's laughter echoed around the house.

Alyssa was now nine months pregnant. Being as young as she was, the only part of her that really seemed pregnant was her stomach— and her arms, legs, and face were still slender, indicating she would slim right up soon after the birth. Janine had enjoyed that, too, as young as she'd been when her girls had been born. Although Carmella was grateful beyond measure to have Georgia and her second pregnancy, she had spoken privately about the difficulties of over-forty pregnancies— the least of which involved losing the baby weight. "But who cares?" Carmella had said. "I'm happy as a clam. My skinny jeans are waiting for me in the back of my closet. Maybe one day I'll see them again."

"My mom is home," Alyssa announced to Nico, smiling as Janine walked through the living room. "Mom, you have to let Nico give you a tour of Teresa's villa. What they've done is extraordinary."

Janine sat next to Alyssa on the couch and waved to Nico, who looked handsome and slightly embarrassed, unsure how to handle the mother of the woman he was clearly smitten with.

"Ciao, Janine! Long time, no see," he said.

"Hi, Nico! Alyssa tells me you've been hard at work," Janine said. "We can't thank you enough for all you've done."

"It's been my pleasure," Nico told her. "And Alyssa's been there every step of the way, as you probably know. I haven't made a single decision without her."

Alyssa beamed.

Nico angled his cell phone out to give Janine a video tour of the first floor of the villa, which had been refurbished, the hardwood polished, new curtains hung, and the walls painted. He explained the way the first floor would be organized into historical eras and that the dining room and kitchen would still be used for museum parties.

"I think Teresa would be very happy to know her kitchen will still be used," Nico said. "It's still a tragedy you were never able to taste her food! It was divine."

Alyssa laughed, her hand over her chest as she gazed at Nico through the screen. Janine had never seen a portrait of such open-hearted love.

And then, all at once, Alyssa's face changed. All the

blood drained from her cheeks, and she gasped, her eyebrows high.

"Oh my gosh! Oh my gosh!" She clutched her neck and stared down at her lap with terror.

"What's going on?" Nico demanded.

But already, Janine understood that Alyssa was going into labor. The baby was on its way. No matter how much Alyssa had tried to pretend that wasn't her reality, the time had come. And she needed to get off the phone.

"I think I have to go?" Alyssa said timidly to Nico. "I think I might have to go to the hospital soon?"

Nico's smile was enormous. "It's happening?"

Alyssa winced. "I think it might be."

"Alyssa, it's going to be fine. It's going to be better than fine!" Nico got closer to the phone, as though he wanted to crawl through. "You're the strongest woman I've ever met."

"I don't feel very strong right now," Alyssa said meekly, her eyes as large as orbs. She stared at Janine, looking more like a little girl than she had in years, then mumbled, "I'll talk to you later, Nico. Okay?"

And swiftly, Alyssa raised her hand, closed the laptop, and burst into tears of fear.

"Come on, honey. It's okay." Janine hugged Alyssa tenderly and said, "Remember what the doctor said. We don't go to the hospital until the contractions are at least five minutes apart, right?"

Alyssa nodded meekly. "I shouldn't have told him what was happening. I should have just pretended I had something else to do."

"Nico knows you pretty well by now," Janine said. "I don't think you can pretend in front of him."

Alyssa curled up into a ball of pain on the couch,

watching an episode of *Friends*, on the hunt for familiarity, as Janine hurried into the kitchen, brewed her a cup of tea, and called Maggie.

Maggie was at The Dog-Eared Corner with Heidi and David, helping at the bakery counter. When she heard the news, she shot into big-sister and mother mode: "I'll be right there."

Over the next few hours, Maggie and Janine did what they could to distract Alyssa from her contractions. They played a game, listened to music, ate snacks, and swapped stories. But all the while, Alyssa's eyes were cloudy, and sweat beads bubbled on her forehead. Around four-thirty that afternoon, they decided it was time to head to the hospital, and Alyssa cried into her hands the entire way as Maggie hugged her in the backseat.

Alyssa was given a sparkling white hospital room with a view of a line of maple trees just outside, which still clung to their autumn leaves, unwilling to give themselves over to the skeletal look of winter. Alyssa changed into a hospital gown and, between spurts of pain, managed to crack a few jokes, which made Janine and Maggie laugh. Throughout these hours, Janine kept in constant contact with the rest of the family, careful to shove away thoughts of Jack, of how he was missing this— the birth of their first grandchild. During their very long marriage, he'd joked about being grandparents together, about growing old and gray together.

And then, for the first time in many months, Janine thought about Maxine.

Immediately after Jack's death, Maxine moved to Martha's Vineyard, and immediately after that, Maxine's long-lost mother moved to Martha's Vineyard, too. But the move hadn't stuck. Although Janine and Maxine still loved one another, even after Maxine and Jack's affair, they'd both entered different phases of their lives— phases in which the other just didn't fit. Janine felt no ill will toward Maxine, especially not now. And when Maxine had told Janine of her and her mother's move to Seattle last spring, Janine had wished Maxine well, grateful to close that chapter of her life.

But now, as Alyssa swam through the terror of her first delivery, Janine remembered Maxine at her bedside during the birth of Maggie, how she'd held her hand, even as Janine had crunched Maxine's to the bone.

During a rare quiet moment in the hospital room, Janine considered whether or not to invite Maxine to her upcoming wedding to Henry. Heavy with thoughts of their past, Janine pulled up Maxine's social media profile to find, to her immense surprise, that Maxine had gotten married just one month ago. The guy was around her age, a father of two teenage boys, and he had a beard that made him look like a lumberjack. In the photographs Maxine had posted, she looked remarkably happy, blissful, even. Janine's heart went out to her, but she did not write her congratulations. That time of their life was over. They'd both made space for something new.

After a long and very painful labor, Alyssa gave birth to a healthy baby boy at four-thirty the following morning — a full twelve hours after they'd left the Remington House. Maggie had held her hand throughout the entire labor, just as Maxine once had for Janine.

"A boy?" Maggie seemed surprised, as though she hadn't been aware someone in their family could have a baby boy rather than a girl.

"A boy!" Alyssa closed her eyes as tears streamed

down her cheeks. "We can name him Leonardo DaVinci!"

Maggie rolled her eyes, which only served to throw several tears down her cheeks, as well. Janine's heart was in her throat. She hardly understood the complexity of her own emotions, as first Alyssa held him, then Maggie—both of them mothers of this spectacular miracle. The way he looked at both of them with such curiosity, his little eyes shining, was captivating. Janine had forgotten what it was like to witness a miracle. Here it was.

Eventually, it was Janine's turn to hold her first grand-child. In her arms, this little boy seemed far too small, impossibly cute, his cheeks red, his ten fingers and ten toes itsy-bitsy. Alyssa had fallen asleep, and only Maggie and Janine were up, ogling him, unable to comprehend him.

"You'll be here soon, Mama," the nurse said to Maggie.

Maggie's eyes bugged out. "All I ever wanted is to be a mother," she told Janine privately after the nurse left. "But that looked painful!"

"You'll be great," Janine assured her, secretly grateful she never had to go through that again.

"Two babies in two months," Maggie whispered. "I can't believe Rex doesn't want anything to do with this little guy!"

"He's an idiot," Janine affirmed.

Just then, at the little window of the hospital door, David's face flashed up, red-cheeked and excited. Apparently, Maggie had finally told him it was okay to come by. Maggie hurried out to say hello, and Janine heard their muffled conversation through the door, with Maggie shrieking with joy. With Alyssa still asleep in bed and the little boy without a name still in Janine's arms, Janine felt as though she had to watch over both of them to protect them.

Around eight o'clock that morning, Janine greeted the rest of the family in the waiting room: Elsa, Carmella, Mallory, Aria, Cole, and Nancy. It seemed like none of them had gotten enough sleep, and they jabbered and over-caffeinated, excited to meet the new member of the family.

"Alyssa just woke up," Janine explained, "and she's going to have breakfast. After that, we can arrange for some visits."

David and Maggie reappeared in the waiting room, returning with coffees and croissants, boisterous with laughter.

"Alyssa requested that lemon-filled croissant from the Frosted Delights Bakery," Maggie said.

"So, we got her three of them," David said. "Just in case."

The waiting room door flung open, and a man whipped through it— his eyes bloodshot and panicked, his clothing disheveled, his jet-black hair in a wild mess behind his ears. When he spotted Janine, he stopped short and began to press his hair down with his hands, looking like a child rather than a man in his late twenties.

"Nico?" Janine and Maggie demanded in unison, absolutely shocked.

Nico's cheeks were blood-red. "Ciao?"

"What are you doing here?" Maggie demanded.

Nico looked unsure of himself, blinking around the waiting room as though he wasn't sure it existed. "Um. I'm here to see Alyssa?"

Maggie and Janine exchanged panicked glances as the

waiting room hushed, all members of the family staring at Nico as though he had four heads. The truth was preposterous— Nico had learned of Alyssa's labor, hopped on a plane, and immediately flown halfway around the world just to make sure she was okay. That was nothing you could ignore.

"I'll show you her room," Janine stuttered, hurrying forward to guide Nico down the hallway. "The baby is asleep, and Alyssa just woke up," she said.

"And she's healthy? Everything went okay?" Nico asked.

Janine turned to look at him. "She did great. Alyssa's healthy. And the baby is a boy! In her medicated state, she suggested the name 'Leonardo DaVinci,' but I don't know if it's going to stick."

Nico cackled, his hand over his stomach as though it hurt. "She's the most hilarious woman I have ever met."

At the hospital door, Janine took a deep breath, knocked on the door, and asked, "Alyssa? You have a surprise visitor. Can I open the door?"

"I hope it's breakfast!" Alyssa called back.

Janine laughed, watching as Maggie hurried forward to pass Nico the bag of croissants. "You can deliver them," Maggie whispered.

Nico nodded, then turned toward the hospital door as though he was facing judgment day. And then, Janine twisted the knob, opened the door, and allowed Nico to enter. After she closed it behind him, she and Maggie walked slowly toward the waiting room, heavy with shock.

"I don't think Alyssa is going to get away with saying they're just friends anymore," Maggie whispered. "Imagine being so loved?"

David stepped up beside Maggie and wrapped his arms around her. "Don't think for a minute I wouldn't do that for you."

Maggie blushed, on the verge of tears again, just as the waiting room door opened with yet another visitor: Henry, who carried yet another bag of baked goods from the Frosted Delights.

"Sorry I'm late," he said, hurrying forward to kiss Janine, allowing her, for the first time in hours, to loosen up, to let someone else take the reins. And in his arms, she felt like water, easing through the bizarre hours of that gorgeous morning, the first day of her grandson's life. There was no telling what would happen next— but he'd had a pretty good start.

Chapter Twenty

And just like that, Martha's Vineyard relinquished its final hold on autumn. A foot of snow fell across the island early one morning, two days before Thanksgiving, capturing those who lived at the Remington House within its walls, at least until Nico found the snow shovel and dug them out. Around that time, Elsa and Bruce rode over on their snowmobile, laden with cookies and packets of hot cocoa, and Elsa hurried inside to dote on the baby, help out with household tasks, and prepare for the upcoming Thanksgiving dinner.

Alyssa and the baby were both happy and healthy. Together, Alyssa and Maggie had decided on a baby name— incredibly, Leo, although Alyssa sometimes liked to call him "DaVinci" to annoy Maggie. Because Maggie was more and more pregnant by the day, and Alyssa less and less, Alyssa did the majority of the baby tasks, falling in love with him. Nico, who still hadn't managed to leave after his spontaneous trip to the United States, was there by her side through all of it. They acted like brand-new parents, and, Janine supposed, they were, in a way. The complications of the way Leo had come into the world didn't matter very much, not now that he was here.

"It's Nico's first Thanksgiving!" Nancy was in the kitchen with a hot cup of cocoa as Elsa sliced onions and a big pot of water heated on the stove. "Those Italians think they're the only ones who know how to cook. We have to prove ourselves."

Elsa cackled as Janine settled on a kitchen chair, poured herself a glass of wine, and watched as the snow floated gently from the sky. It was no longer as thick as it had been, and they probably wouldn't get many more inches— but it was not giving up.

"I hope Lucy and Hunter can still make it in for Thanksgiving," Janine said.

"We need Lucy here," Elsa agreed. "Gosh, can you imagine how much she's changed since August? At that age, every day is a new adventure."

"Leo's already changed so much since he was born," Nancy said with a sigh. "Every time I look at him, his face looks a little less chubby to me. It breaks my heart!"

Elsa eyed Janine curiously. "Still no word from Rex after the birth?"

Janine shook her head. "I think Maggie prefers it that way. She's up to her ears in babies and love. Rex is just a reminder of everything that went wrong."

A few minutes later, Nico appeared in the kitchen with a swaddled baby Leo in his arms. Unlike how he'd been in Italy, always dressed to the nines for his museum tour guide job, he now wore a pair of Boston College sweatpants and a big t-shirt, his hair floppy from lazing around the house.

"Ciao!" Nancy greeted him. "Can we get you anything? Tea? Wine?"

"No, no." Nico laughed and cradled Leo gently. "I'm just taking Leo for a little walk around the house. It's all we can do right now."

"The snow's gorgeous, isn't it?" Janine asked.

"It's stunning," Nico said, sounding wistful. "I sent photographs to my family in Italy, and they lost their minds."

That night, Elsa and Nancy made everyone homemade pizzas, which they ate on the floor or the couch of the living room, sprawled out as a Christmas movie played on the television. Nobody really paid attention to it and instead chatted with one another or stared out the window. Leo was asleep in his crib upstairs, still in the cozy era of being too young to stay awake longer than a few hours a day.

"Enjoy this time," Janine told Alyssa. "Pretty soon, he'll want to be a part of the world."

When Alyssa and Janine were in the kitchen at the same time, grabbing glasses of water, Janine managed to corner her to ask her a question that had been heavy on her mind.

"What's going on with the museum?"

Alyssa waved her hand. "We're taking care of it."

"What do you mean?"

Alyssa looked her dead in the eye. "Nico talks to the crew every day on the phone to see how it's going. The museum staff he already hired is going through Teresa's things for more artifacts. Everything is right on time."

Janine was amazed. She'd thought the pair of them were lost in baby-time— but they'd been strong-arming the refurbishment of a museum half the world away.

"I guess that means nothing is dragging Nico back to Italy any time soon," Janine said.

Alyssa's cheeks were pink. "We haven't talked about when he's leaving."

"If he ever leaves."

Alyssa gave her mother a look. It was clear she didn't want to consider his leaving, nor did she want to have that conversation. She was caught up in the most gorgeous time of her life with a new baby, a new love, and a new career in museum work, all blossoming at once.

Just before Janine left the kitchen, Alyssa took her shoulder and said, "Mom?"

"What is it, honey?"

"It's nice being in love. Isn't it?" Alyssa laughed at herself as she let her hand drop. "I don't think I knew it would be half this nice."

Janine was overwhelmed with thousands of images of her own love story, like the first time she'd seen Jack in that bar, or the first day of Maggie's life, followed by Alyssa's. She thought of when she and Maxine had met one another back in elementary school, both lost girls from Brooklyn, without two pennies to rub together, then considered the first time she'd ever seen Henry, when her heart had been broken, and she'd been unsure if she had the strength to put it back together again.

"It makes everything else worth it, doesn't it?" Janine breathed.

* * *

By the morning of Thanksgiving, Martha's Vineyard had cleared its roads, and the skies had calmed enough to allow Hunter and Lucy to fly into Boston and take the ferry to the island. To Janine's immense surprise, when she walked into the kitchen that morning for a mug of coffee, she found none other than Stan Ellis over the stove, wearing an apron and stirring several different dishes.

"Your mother has me hard at work," he explained timidly.

Nancy bustled into the kitchen, her arms ladened with dishes. "Janine! Good morning! Happy Thanksgiving!"

Janine gave her mother a confused smile. Why was Stan here? Nancy had always had a soft spot for him, especially after he'd saved her during that hurricane. But was there something else going on?

Janine poured herself a cup of coffee, leaned against the counter, and asked, "Can I help you with something?"

Nancy's voice remained bright. She knew exactly what she was doing, what kind of curiosity she was creating. "Let's see," she said, heading for the stovetop, where she placed her hand on Stan's lower back! Janine blinked several times, gobsmacked. "I don't think we need any help right now," Nancy assured her. "You made the pies yesterday, right?"

"That was mostly Maggie," Janine admitted. "But she let me help."

Nancy laughed and leaned against Stan, clearly very easy around him. It was plain as anything that they were lovers. *When had it happened?*

Not long afterward, Henry arrived at the Remington House, bringing with him numerous bottles of wine. His kisses were chilly from the wicked east coast temperatures, but his hugs were warm, and Janine cuddled against him in the empty living room, listening as Nancy and Stan laughed in the kitchen.

"Mom's in love," she whispered to Henry. "And she's kept it a secret!"

Henry laughed. "Good for her. It was time."

"I think you're right about that."

Lucy and Hunter arrived around eleven, when the Remington House was already filled with family members, each of them squabbling or gossiping, drinking coffee, or already snacking. When the doorbell rang, Alyssa hurried to answer it, and then, Lucy was suddenly running around the house, greeting everyone excitedly, hugging their legs, calling their names. Hunter brought up the rear, smiling good-naturedly with that dimple he'd always had since boyhood. He shook Nico's hand and doted on baby Leo as Lucy continued to act as though she ruled the house. For a time, she had.

Although Maggie was now six months pregnant, she managed to have Lucy on her lap for much of the early afternoon, the hours before Thanksgiving dinner, and her eyes were enormous with love for the little girl. Lucy talked at length about her preschool out in Seattle and how beautiful the mountains were, and nobody could quite believe how eloquent she was, as she was only three and a half years old. Hunter just laughed and said she'd clearly gotten it all from the Remington-Potter-Grimson girls. "You changed her life," he said to them unabashedly, and nobody corrected him.

When it was time to sit down for dinner, everyone gathered around the massive table, which they'd stuffed with as many chairs as they could. Across from Janine sat Aria, her mother, Bethany, and Cole, and next to her sat Henry and Maggie, with Alyssa and Nico just a few seats over. Nancy and Stan sat next to one another at one of the heads of the table, holding hands between their plates. It was as though they always had to be touching.

"I think we should make some kind of toast," Nancy announced. "Our say a prayer."

"I'll start," Stan said, his voice wavering as he raised his glass of wine and closed his eyes— not sure if he was praying or toasting. Maybe he was doing his best. "I just want to thank God above for bringing me into this beautiful and welcoming family. I was lost for so many years. And I don't know if I deserve the love I've recently found... But my goodness, I'll take it."

After that, Maggie spoke. "And I want to thank God for my sister, who brought Leo into the world. It's been a complicated, tumultuous year, but Leo is gorgeous and healthy, and I'm over the moon. Besides that..." Maggie eyed David beside her, "I want to thank God for bringing David and Heidi into my life. Heidi's bookstore completely changed my professional trajectory, and David's love completely shaped my view of the world." Maggie swallowed and then turned her attention to Janine, who hardly kept it together as Maggie added, "And of course, I want to thank my mother for loving me, for being there for me in everything, and for taking Alyssa and I on that wild goose chase to Italy. I'll remember those golden weeks forever."

The thanks continued— words spoken over that glowing table, laden with a glistening turkey, stuffing, freshly-baked rolls, sweet potatoes, butter layered with shards of salt, Brussels sprouts cooked in white wine, mashed potatoes, and gravy— and even more helpings of other varieties of sides, of a tofu dish Elsa's youngest daughter had made because she'd decided to be a vegetarian this month. And in the kitchen sat heaps of pies, cakes, brownies, and lemon bars, all lying in wait for a long afternoon of sipping wine, of second and third helpings of desserts and conversation. Janine's heart swelled in expectation for all of it. She just prayed it wouldn't go too quickly.

Chapter Twenty-One

For a very long time back in Manhattan, Maggie's doctors had told her she probably would never be able to conceive. Perhaps due to this doubt, when Maggie went into labor one month ahead of schedule, during a Christmas shopping extravaganza with Janine on December 17th, she fully panicked.

"The baby's too early," Maggie whispered, wincing in pain in the front seat of Janine's car as she drove them to the hospital.

"Only three and a half weeks," Janine told her. "That's nothing. Really."

"Too early," Maggie whimpered. "It's not time."

"The baby looked really healthy at your last appointment!" Janine reminded her. "And you've read it over and over again in your baby books. This is a fine time to bring the baby into the world. And you've been so uncomfortable, Maggie. It'll finally be over!"

But Maggie was very good at worrying, and the early delivery had brought a new dimension to that worry. Unlike the other babies, the ones she'd lost in a number of miscarriages, this baby felt far more real— and Maggie was terrified that she'd counted her blessings before they'd hatched.

Maggie's hospital room was just a few doors from the one Alyssa had delivered Leo in. Her face drawn, she sat at the edge of the bed and stared at the floor, willing David to get here soon. All the while, Janine did her best to talk her daughter down, to remind her that she had a very good doctor, that she and the baby were healthy.

In truth, Janine was very pleased when David appeared at the door, ready with kind words and kisses. The pair of them hadn't been together much longer than that embryo had been implanted (the natural way, this time), but they'd built a gorgeous relationship together, one of trust and understanding. And when Maggie looked at David, Janine allowed herself a sigh of relief— and stepped into the waiting room to give them some space.

Not long after Janine left the delivery room, Alyssa, Nico, and baby Leo arrived at the hospital. As Nico held Leo gently, Alyssa threw her arms around her mother, saying, "Maggie must be freaking out."

"Oh, she is," Janine told her.

"But three and a half weeks early isn't bad!"

"I told her that," Janine said.

"She doesn't like to listen to reason."

"You know her better than anyone," Janine offered.

"We both do," Alyssa said.

For the majority of the labor and delivery, Maggie and David kept to themselves— with Maggie infrequently asking for her sister or mother to come in to say hello. Eventually, Henry came by the hospital with sandwiches, and Nico brought Leo back to the Remington House so that they could both sleep more comfortably. Still, Alyssa and Janine remained, pacing the halls of the hospital, and talking, talking, talking.

"How does it feel?" Janine asked Alyssa, sometime past midnight, after six or so hours of Maggie's labor. "To be a mother?"

Alyssa pondered this for a moment. "Everything is in flux right now, you know? Because Leo is technically Maggie's. But she's been so tired with her own pregnancy and nervous about this next step..."

"Having two little ones?"

Alyssa nodded. "But Nico and I have talked about having a baby of our own. And I'm not averse to that at all."

Janine was surprised. "So soon?"

"No, no," Alyssa said, waving her hands. "I talked to Maggie last week about all of this. The plan is that Nico and I will go back to Italy later this year when Leo doesn't need me as much anymore. We'll be there for the last months of the museum refurbishment, and we'll help as it opens up for good."

"Wow." Janine's heart filled with hope for them, for what they could accomplish together.

"I was so convinced that I could just stay at the Remington House, to be with Leo and Maggie forever," Alyssa said. "But it's true that I found my footing in Venice."

"I've never seen you like that," Janine said.

"I never really knew who I was or what I wanted," Alyssa said softly. "And Teresa's will showed me."

"And it brought you to Nico."

"Can you believe that?" Alyssa shook her head.

"I always knew that amazing things would happen in

yours and Maggie's lives," Janine admitted. "But everything that did is beyond my wildest dreams."

* * *

Maggie's healthy baby girl was born at seven that morning as the first light of the December morning seeped through the dying grass along the sands of the island. When David erupted from the hospital room to announce the baby and mother's health, he wept into his hands and hugged his mother, Heidi. For years, Heidi had been all by herself in that bookstore, battling a debilitating mental disease. And now, here she was at the hospital, welcoming her first grandchild, tears in her eyes as she asked everyone if they wanted a coffee from the machine. If she should order donuts. If anyone had extra makeup in their purse, as she wanted to look okay during the photographs with the baby.

Not long after the baby's birth, Alyssa and Janine were allowed in the room to meet the darling girl. Because Alyssa and Maggie had named Leo together, Maggie insisted that Alyssa help her with the baby girl's name— and Alyssa threw ridiculous names at her, ones that made a very tired Maggie bubble with laughter.

"You'll never take anything seriously, will you?" she demanded.

"Gosh, I hope not," Alyssa said, gazing down at the beautiful baby in her arms.

* * *

Three days after the baby's birth and four before Christmas, the Remington House was full yet again to welcome baby Lorelei to the world. Nobody could get enough of her, of her tiny toes and her little fingers and her ringlet curls, and Christmas music hummed from speakers across the ground floor as another snowfall floated down outside.

Janine was lucky enough to hold both of her grandchildren every single day of that holiday season— alternating between Leo and his bright blue eyes and Lorelei and her dark brown ones, carefully changing diapers and cradling them as they slept. Both Maggie and Alyssa thanked her over and over again for her help, but Janine wasn't sure where in the world she'd rather be.

But that afternoon, as the Remington family stood around the house, eating Christmas cookies and doting on Leo and Lorelei, Maggie broke the big news.

"David and I want to find a place to live. Somewhere outside the Remington House."

Janine, Nancy, and Alyssa were the only ones within earshot, scattered across the Remington House kitchen. It struck Janine, at this moment, that she'd been living at the Remington House for two and a half years at this point, that life had whipped past her like a runaway train. It was time for Maggie to move on.

"No," Nancy said then, her jaw set.

"But Grandma, it's time," Maggie said, her eyes soft and apologetic.

"That's not what I mean," Nancy said, drying her hands on a towel. "I don't want to live here anymore. I think it's time you, Alyssa, and the babies took over."

Maggie's jaw dropped. Even Janine looked at her mother, flabbergasted. For many years, this had been Nancy's home, her refuge after a terrifically difficult childhood, teenage era, and adulthood. But she'd dragged her way out of the mess and wound up here. It was truly remarkable. Why would she give it up?

"Don't look at me like that," Nancy said. "I love this house. I love the memories I've made in it. But it's too big for just me."

"But where will you go, Grandma?" Alyssa asked.

Nancy's eyes sparkled. "You should really see Stan's place. He's made it into something really special. A home. It's small, yes— more like a cottage by the sea. But after where I came from in Brooklyn, it's a palace. And it's all I need, honestly." She paused for a moment before adding, "And it's not too much to clean, thank goodness."

"When are you going to move in with Stan?" Maggie asked.

"Maybe soon," Nancy said with a shrug. "I love helping out around here, and I want to come as much as I'm needed. But I know I'm mostly in the way right now, what with all the babies and everything. Besides, I know you want to raise the babies side-by-side. This house is big enough for an arrangement like that. It's a mini-mansion, for goodness' sake. Fill it with children!"

Unsure what to say, Maggie cleared the distance between them, wrapped her arms around her grandmother, and waved for Alyssa to join them. She did, calling for Janine. Together, the three generations of Grimson-Potter gals group-hugged in the kitchen of Neal Remington's house so many years after he'd first purchased it. And, Janine knew, the familiar heartbeat of the house would go forth, becoming stronger as Maggie and Alyssa took hold of it and made it their own.

Chapter Twenty-Two

On Christmas Eve morning, Nancy brought three suitcases to Stan Ellis' cottage with the plan to never leave him. "Three suitcases?" had been the way Alyssa, Maggie, and Janine had exclaimed it, as though Nancy had lost her dang mind—but Nancy had been adamant. For all those years living with Neal, she'd accrued far too much stuff, and she, a woman who'd come from nothing, was ready to return to nothing. It was nice.

Stan, being Stan, helped Nancy hang up her dresses, put away her jeans, and put her socks and underwear in the top drawer on the other side of his. As Nancy watched her things fill out the rest of his space, her heart filled up with love, and she collapsed on the mattress (which she'd purchased for Stan's place, as her back wasn't what it once was) and cuddled Stan close. At some point that morning, he convinced her to come to the kitchen, where he surprised her with a fresh batch of blueberry pancakes and coffee, and they watched the snow fall down over the ocean. This deep in her sixties,

Nancy hadn't envisioned such happiness for herself. Yet here it was.

"Would you like another pancake?" Stan asked.

"I have no space left in my stomach, but I can't say no."

Although Nancy had plans with the rest of her family on Christmas Day, she'd decided to spend the entire Christmas Eve with Stan, which thrilled him to no end. The pancakes were just the tip of the iceberg in terms of food, as he'd apparently plotted a multi-course, day-long event with Greek, French, and Italian-inspired dishes that nearly brought Nancy to her knees.

Around four-thirty, Stan's ex-stepson, Tommy, came over with his wife, Lola Sheridan— the youngest daughter of Anna— and the four of them sat around the Christmas tree for an hour, catching up, before Lola and Tommy were needed with the rest of the Sheridan family at the Sunrise Cove Inn. Lola was a classic bohemian with long hair, an open smile, and eager curiosity, proof she'd worked as a wonderful journalist throughout her career.

"You must have some kind of secret power, Nancy," Lola said. "I would have never imagined Stan would put up a Christmas tree. Not in a million years."

"We picked it out together," Nancy said, blushing at the memory of that snow-filled afternoon a few weeks ago, when Stan had brought his ax from the garage, and he'd hacked down Nancy's favorite Christmas tree at the Christmas tree farm outside of Oaks Bluff. Stan had dragged the tree back to the truck, and together, they'd tied it up, their hair filling with snowflakes. It was a level of domesticity Stan had probably only dreamed of.

When Tommy and Lola left, Stan hugged his ex-stepson extra long and waved as Tommy backed his truck out of the driveway. Nancy watched him with her heart in her throat. Who was this man? And how had she gotten so lucky to know him?

For dinner, Stan had planned a feast: honey-glazed ham, asparagus, yams, and freshly baked bread. For dessert, he'd put together a remarkable cheese plate with camembert, brie, an aged gouda, a roquefort, and a Norwegian cheese that tasted a bit like caramel. Stan opened up a beautiful bottle of French wine, which he poured a small portion of into Nancy's glass, pretending to be a waiter at a fancy restaurant. Nancy sipped, nodded her head, and said, "Monsieur, it's marvelous!"

"Trés bien is how we say it," Stan joked, feigning a French accent.

As they ate, Nancy couldn't help but be nostalgic. And, because Stan was a wonderful listener, he allowed her to fall into her worlds of memories, thinking back to the Christmases when she'd been a girl.

"All the other kids got presents, you know. But I always knew that wasn't coming, not for me. And my daddy always got so drunk on Christmas Eve. Drunk and sad. Oh, it hurt me so much when he got like that." Nancy sighed and scraped her fork over her yams. "It's insane to me how long ago that was. I've turned into an old woman."

Stan reached for her hand and slid his thumb over hers. Her heart hummed with yearning.

"You don't look old to me," Stan said.

"Maybe we should get you a new prescription for your glasses."

Stan laughed, opening his mouth wider to show his healthy, white teeth, his shoulders shaking. Nancy thought again of Anna, all those years ago, when she'd been frustrated in her marriage and sought refuge here, with him. But Nancy wasn't seeking refuge with Stan. She was building a life with him. There was a difference.

"I'm so happy to live in a house like this," Nancy said spontaneously.

"What? Are you joking? That house you were in was a mansion! It was beautiful."

"Exactly. When I was growing up, and even later, into my forties, I always lived in little places. I loved it, feeling like I was tucked away in my hiding place as the big world went on without me."

"What did living in such a big house feel like?" Stan asked.

"Like I said before," Nancy breathed, "I felt like a ghost in that place sometimes. Like I was living in someone else's house, walking the hallways, feeling lost."

"I hope you won't feel lost here," Stan said.

Nancy squeezed his hand. "I've never felt lost with you. I always know exactly who I am and where we stand." She frowned, surprising herself with how open she felt. "And that's a very rare thing, you know?"

"I know," Stan said, kissing her hand. "I've felt misunderstood all my life— by the world and by myself."

"I hope those days are over."

"I think they finally are," he said, his eyes shining.

Chapter Twenty Three

Janine stood over two cribs. To the left slept Leo, born November 8th, and to the right slept Lorelei, born December 18th. Remarkably, neither of them had stirred for two hours, leaving the Remington House (or was it the Potter House?) in silence. It was New Year's Eve, the final day in what had been a truly sensational year. And Grandma Janine was babysitting.

Downstairs, Janine found Henry in front of the television with a beer and several bowls of snacks filled with peanuts, pita chips, and pretzels, along with several types of spreads, including hummus, spinach and artichoke dip, and cheese. On the surface, it looked as though they'd over-prepped for just the two of them, but they knew that, before midnight, Nico, Alyssa, David, and Maggie would return home to celebrate the ball drop together as a family. With them there, the food would be gone in no time flat.

In the silence, Janine cuddled up against Henry, watching as Quentin Copperfield and a co-host spoke on television in Times Square, introducing musical guests and counting down the hours till 2024.

"Three suitcases," Janine repeated, thinking again of her mother's big move to Stan's.

"I doubt you'll be able to make that happen," Henry teased her, kissing her on the ear.

Janine laughed and wrapped her arms around her knees. "You should have seen the closet space I had in Manhattan. Walk-in closet after walk-in closet. I felt like the queen of the Upper West Side. For a while, I really was."

Henry raised his eyebrows.

"I don't regret leaving that world in the slightest," Janine hurried to add, nodding toward Quentin. "As you know, Quentin raised his family just down the street from mine. I remember so many afternoons dropping Alyssa or Maggie off with Scarlet for ballet or tutoring or cello or whatever they were doing that week. He was always off work early since he started at three or four in the morning. And always, there was this breathless quality to both of us, as though we just couldn't catch ourselves. We were running a race in the Upper West Side. And we were always, always going to lose it."

Henry rubbed Janine's shoulders, sensing her tension as though the past had come up to stress her out again.

"Anyway, my point is, I'm out of there now. I have the freedom to create a whole new era with you. And yeah. I don't need those walk-in closets anymore."

"But you don't have to get rid of everything like your mother did. Just ease into it. I know you'll want to spend a lot of time here with the babies. Move your stuff a little bit at a time. At some point, we'll find ourselves up to our ears in your dresses. But it won't be soon."

Janine laughed and wrapped her arms around him again, inhaling his comforting smell. On television, Quentin was talking about the highs of 2023— a year that, she knew, had nearly taken his wife from him. But it hadn't. And he'd left Manhattan, together with his family, to start anew in Nantucket. Janine understood that better than anyone.

Maggie, David, Alyssa, and Nico had gone out to a New Year's Eve party at the Aquinnah Cliffside Overlook Hotel— a remarkable, 1920s-themed party, where Alyssa and Maggie had dressed like flappers from one hundred years ago, and David and Nico had donned suits. The photographs they took and posted to social media that night featured them as beautiful people at the very beginning of their lives. And, despite all the messes they'd made and all the ways they felt they were "so old," they really *were* at the beginning. There was so much living left.

The issue of Leo was a tricky one. He was Maggie and Rex's, biologically— but Alyssa had carried him and birthed him, and Nico had fallen head-over-heels with him. They'd decided that when Alyssa and Nico went back to Italy to open the museum, they would make the hard decisions about his "legal parents." Until then, and even after, they would shower him with as much love as they could muster.

With Maggie's marriage to Rex officially finished, Rex had married his new beau— posting a smattering of photographs on the internet, some of which Maggie and

Alyssa flicked through in the bathroom at the Aquinnah Cliffside Overlook Hotel.

"This is dumb," Alyssa insisted. "We shouldn't look at these."

"It honestly doesn't hurt me to see," Maggie said. "I just find it bizarre. Who would have guessed the stories would have played out like this?"

At eleven that night, a full hour before the night transitioned to the next year, a sober David drove them back to the Remington House to find Henry and Janine half-asleep on the couch, surrounded by snacks. Alyssa and Maggie leaped on the couch, like children, to wake them up, and Janine screamed as Henry cackled with laughter. Nico and David immediately dove into the snacks, scraping the bottom of the bowl for as much hummus as they could, as Janine reminded them there was "a lot more hummus in the fridge."

At eleven-thirty, the doorbell rang again to reveal Nancy and Stan, who carried in three bottles of champagne and tiny homemade cupcakes slathered with frosting. Nancy threw open her arms to hug everyone as, upstairs, Leo and Lorelei woke up, wailing for their mothers and fathers, for all the love they were given in that enormous home. Alyssa and Maggie scampered up to get them and returned with the babies in their arms, laughing. Upstairs, as they'd lifted them up, they'd shared a private conversation, in which Alyssa had asked, "How early is it to get pregnant again?" and Maggie had said, "Pregnant again? Are you insane?" And they'd laughed about how their roles had been reversed, how, once upon a time, all Maggie had wanted was to have baby after baby, to fill her life with little ones. Now, Alyssa was following her lead.

When the ball dropped in Times Square, and everyone on Eastern Standard Time, across the eastern seaboard, and across the island of Martha's Vineyard opened their champagne bottles and celebrated the first moments of a brand-new year, everyone in the Remington House hugged and kissed and drank, overzealous with the energy of hope.

"My first year in the United States!" Nico said, raising his glass for a refill. Already, he'd begun the process of getting an American visa so that he could stay by Alyssa's side as long as possible.

"And this is the year we'll get married," Janine said, leaning against Henry.

"Us, too," Stan announced bashfully, gazing at Nancy as though he couldn't believe his luck.

"Us, too!" David laughed and tugged Maggie against him.

Only Nico and Alyssa remained quiet, eyeing one another, stifling their laughter.

"What are you two keeping from us?" Maggie demanded.

And then, because Alyssa was Alyssa and always would be spontaneous, wild, and free, she removed her wedding ring from her pocket, slid it on her finger, and said, "We got married yesterday. At the courthouse."

Immediately, everyone shrieked with excitement and shock.

"That's what you were doing yesterday afternoon?" Janine demanded. "When you asked me to babysit? And you didn't tell me!"

"It's just easier that way!" Alyssa cried, trying to push off the drama of it all. "He can stay in the United States. We can both work at the museum abroad. It's easy!"

But the Potter-Grimson girls wouldn't let up on their enthusiasm. More champagne was opened, and more hummus was fetched. Janine again demanded why they hadn't told her, even though she thought she probably understood. Alyssa, being Alyssa, was private, romantic, and secretive. She adored the drama of an elopement— and she'd created a story she could truly believe in with Nico.

In fact, that's what they were all doing— Janine, Nancy, Alyssa, Maggie, and even the rest of them, Elsa and Carmella and their children, all people Janine had fallen completely in love with over the years. They were all good-hearted, kind, and wonderful in ways Janine could hardly put into words. And all they were doing, every day, was fighting for their personal stories, their personal happily ever afters. In such a mysterious and complicated world, it was all they could do.

Dear Readers

I wanted to let you know that I've decided to retire the Katama Bay Series. This will allow me to focus on plotting a new series that, of course, will be women's fiction that will deal with many family issues. I've loved writing about the Potter and Remington ladies, and you just never know— I many find the time to write a spin off or an additional couple books in my free time next year. For now, though, Katama will be a closed chapter and I thank you so much for supporting this series.

If you haven't read my Sister's of Edgartown, you should absolutely check it out. This series is also set on Martha's Vineyard and deals with many family issues that I think you'll love.

Start Reading 2152 Green Hollow RD

Dear Readers

Other Books by Katie

The Vineyard Sunset Series
Sisters of Edgartown Series
Secrets of Mackinac Island Series
A Katama Bay Series
A Mount Desert Island Series
A Nantucket Sunset Series
The Coleman Series

Made in the USA
Monee, IL
23 April 2024

57373963R00108